wishes,

Patty Stone

Nov 9/91

Close Calls

short stories
by

Patricia Stone

Patricia Stone.

Cormorant Books

Published with the assistance of the Canada Council and the Ontario Arts Council.

The author would like to acknowledge the following magazines and periodicals where some of this material has appeared: *Cross-Canada Writers' Magazine Short Story Contest* (first prize for "Passing On"), *The Antigonish Review*, *event*, *The New Quarterly*, and *Matrix*. "Living on the Lake" has been included in *Journey Prize Anthology*, published by McClelland & Stewart in 1991.

Cover from an oil on canvas, *Brambles II*, by D.C. Walker, (1985, 125 x 153.5 cm) courtesy of the artist and the Canada Council Art Bank.

Printed and bound in Canada.

Published by
Cormorant Books
RR 1
Dunvegan, Ontario
K0C 1J0

Canadian Cataloguing in Publication Data

Stone, Patricia, 1952-

Close calls

ISBN 0-920953-62-X

I. Title.

PS8587.T66C46 1991   C813' .54   C91-090415-4
PR9199.3.S86C46 1991

Table of Contents

Passing On

Nan Adams sat in the bathtub and solemnly stared at her toe. The cut had gotten redder during the day, and now through the tepid water, her toe seemed to be taking on a strange colour. This is blood poisoning, Nan heard herself thinking. The truth made her feel heavy and sick. She had suspected for two days—ever since dropping the knife she had been using to divide an orange for breakfast on Tuesday. The sharp side of the blade had hit her foot and the blood bounced up like a small geyser.

Propping her foot up, Nan turned on the tap. She endured a jet of hot water on her toe until it almost scalded her—then cold, till goosebumps stood up on her leg. Maybe the contrast of hot and cold would fix things.

"Nan, what in God's name are you doing in there?" Mrs. Adams called from the kitchen.

Nan stiffened. "I'm just keeping the bath from going cold," she said loudly, taken aback at hearing her voice sound normal—horrified at her lie, at putting off the moment when she would have to tell her parents.

"Well, be careful, or you'll use up all the hot water on your father."

Nan remained motionless for a few minutes, not daring to lower her foot; even a splash might attract her mother's investigation. She would march right into the bathroom—no one was allowed to lock the door—see the injured toe and that would be the end of putting off the inevitable. "Will it have to be amputated?" Nan asked herself. Dread began to beat in her stomach and throat till dark spots danced before her eyes.

"I could pray to God if he would listen; but I know there isn't one and if there is, he'll see that I'm praying without truly believing it will work."

For a moment, she sat and gazed bleakly at the tiles on the wall. Then she decided to pray anyhow and covered her eyes with her hands.

"God, save my toe, don't let me have blood poisoning; please make me better this one time and I swear I'll never ask you again to. . . . "

She stopped then. She couldn't promise that.

And she wondered how life would feel if she wasn't always afraid that death was near and waiting. She had watched and had seen that most people did not seem to worry about their lives being cut short by sudden death. Even old people went about looking cheerful, as if they never spent a second thinking about the bewildering black void so near them.

It would be nice, Nan thought, not to have to worry all the time about dying.

She did not care so much for herself—death would probably not affect her. But she couldn't bear the thought of her family having to live on afterwards, their faces always falling away from a smile. None of them would ever be able to laugh again if Nan died. And she passionately hated the idea of her mother who sometimes repeated in a grim, strangled voice, "I don't know what I'd do if anything ever happened to one of you kids."

Despite what the Bible said and what the minister's wife taught at Sunday School, Nan didn't really believe in Heaven. For a while, she had been half-convinced that there was a God, an omnipotent loving father, overseeing things. Then a new idea had occurred to her: a God who was the original creator did not necessarily have a heaven to offer. Nevertheless, she went to church, alone, every Sunday, enjoying the feeling of self-discipline it gave her. She was fond of the illustrated Bible books that revealed heaven to be a glorious, flaming opening cloud of brilliant colour. A small curious side of her was partial to the idea of a "life hereafter". To Nan, the promise of life after death had overtones of fairy tales she especially enjoyed: tales with eerie but happy endings.

Her mother had sung in the choir once but did not feel up to going to church anymore. The church had "let her down". Not that the Adams had ever been fanatical where religion was concerned—not like the Catholics where the priest ruled the family and forced the women to have children even if it cost them their lives finally. "If you ever marry a Catholic, I'll jump in Lake Ontario," Mrs. Adams had said one afternoon, sitting in her chair. Nan was cross-legged on the floor bent over a comic book. They had been discussing religion again; and then, Mrs. Adams launched into her favourite "Dogan" story, about sewers plugged in Montreal during March and men going down and discovering the bodies of half-formed babies in the drains emerging from the nunneries. "So there's a priest for you," Mrs. Adams would say at the conclusion of her story. Because she hated choir practice, Mrs. Adams quit the choir; and when she had stomached enough talk of "crosses to bear" and "God works in strange ways", she quit the United Church completely.

So Nan went to the services by herself and felt proud and worthy, even though she often used the time to daydream during the sermons and to eat peppermints kept in her coat pocket. On deep winter mornings, when the house was still cold, and there were only the sounds of her father getting ready for work and her mother stirring oatmeal before the school bus arrived, Nan sat beside the heater vent in her bedroom and listened to the snow matting itself against the storm windows and the deep hoarse wind in the fields beyond the house, while she read her copy of the New Testament—a chapter a day, searching, trying to figure things out. But the stories were, page after page, unintelligible. Nan lost a truth as soon as she had discerned one. She couldn't understand herself since generally she memorized things quickly. And nowhere had she learned the truth about dying.

More than once Nan had thought about killing herself, about getting the thing over with—but she didn't think about that now sitting in the cooling water and looking at the swollen toe. She was not sure why she ever thought about committing suicide—except that the nearness of death felt unbearable. She was terrified of her own life because it meant dying; and she knew that, somehow, this was connected with her mother's constant sighs about the inevitability of dying and her conversations about how relatives had died—ancient family secrets that were like nursery songs whose words had been forgotten but whose tune lingered intact.

One afternoon the summer before, Mrs. Adams had taken Nan and the two boys to the cemetery so the children might see the plots in which she and Father were to be buried someday. It was a practical thing to do. "So this is where you'll be pushing up daisies," Danny had joked. Nan and her other brother had laughed out loud until they saw the look on their mother's face. Afterwards, Nan had visions of coffins frozen into wintery ground and the wet oozing spring mud, and the insects that might get inside—the kind that were black and shiny and wet beneath overturned logs. But sometimes she amused herself by rehearsing scenes where she was dead, having a funeral, and people remembered what they had said or done and were sorry. She hoped for the power of invisibility after death so that she could watch the reactions.

Nan turned on the water and let it run till the bath

9

was very hot again.

Mrs. Adams rapped on the door. "Have you drowned in there?"

"No, I'm getting out now." Nan let her leg drop into the water and it thudded on the ceramic bottom. She winced as she stood up.

Mrs. Adams was listening. There was a hushed, expectant silence in the hallway.

Nan sat on the toilet lid and began to dry her feet so that if her mother came in, she could hide the toe. It was unfair not being allowed to lock the bathroom door; a person did not feel private. But Mrs. Adams said all kinds of things could go wrong—you could panic and drown in an inch of water; there were cases of this happening described in the newspapers and on the radio. Or if a storm leaped up, you had to get out of the tub fast since lightning not only struck through open screens and along telephone wires, but there was even a case somewhere in the United States where the lightning had gone right through the plumbing of some man's house into the tub where he was taking a bath. At least it would have been a quick death. "Wouldn't know what hit him," Mrs. Adams had said in a tone that was sorry and pleased.

Nan heard her mother's slippers slap down the hall to the living room.

Once, they were giving out tuberculosis tests at school. Nan had been sure that she would faint and everyone would witness her cowardice. She did not faint, but when Nan's circle of pin pricks remained red a day after her test, Mrs. Adams said, "You just might have TB—that could just be a year in a sanitorium."

Her mother was normally quite calm when she made her preliminary diagnosis which meant that Nan, as well, had to keep up a show when inside she felt paralyzed, and she knew that her mother felt the same but neither could admit it.

On another occasion, when she had a pain in her leg for several days, Mrs. Adams said it was likely rheumatic fever—girls who were Nan's age tended to get it, and a girl could be left crippled unless she had strict bed-rest for six months. Both times, when she lay in bed at night thinking about TB and then rheumatic fever, Nan could not decide whether she would enjoy being that sick or not. A period of recuperation meant candy and gifts and cards in the mail, days of reading and daydreaming. But even the closest relatives forgot you were sick after a few days. Whenever she was thirsty after being in the woods all afternoon or out in the street with the other kids, she never let on to her mother and tried to avoid drinking because once her mother had explained that excessive thirst was a symptom of sugar diabetes—and that meant insulin injections.

Nan had a terror of needles. All the Adams did—although not Nan's father, of course, who seemed to be different from the rest of them, cheerful, unconcerned. Frequently, there were unavoidable appointments with the doctor for boosters and other annual shots. "You'll be all right," Mrs. Adams would say in a unbelieving, too-kind way, and a look always passed over her face that made Nan feel suddenly engulfed by silent grim tears and even the nurse would look uncomfortable. Just the sight of the Doctor's Office and the smell of tongue depressors and disinfectant, and the nurses with never a wrinkle, and the *Children's Collection of Bible Stories* on the waiting-room table made Nan's heart race. The greatest fear was of being bitten by a mad dog and having to undergo the terrible Rabies Series which, according to Nan's mother, were the most painful needles on earth—right into the stomach. Nan had made a pact with herself that if a mad squirrel or cat ever bit her—and she would know by its foaming mouth—she would definitely kill herself.

There was always the possibility of untimely, tragic

death. She had never realized so clearly how dying preoccupied her until one afternoon. She had been coming up from the woods after running all day along the paths pretending to be galloping on an unbroken black stallion; and then to be running faster than anyone had ever run before, down hills never losing her footing. She was coming home, crossing yards to follow one of the secret routes she had invented—and for no reason, she had frozen. In between the white slat fence that lined a neighbour's driveway down the street—as she was climbing through that white fence—she had stopped. It was as if the whole world clicked off, jarred to a sickeningly permanent halt for just an instant—and she thought of death again.

She knew then how final it was, how the thought would always affect her life. After that one moment when she stopped moving at the fence, and ever since, Nan kept wondering about her body and about her mother's unending knowledge of diseases. It was a fact, Mrs. Adams said, that when people died and underwent autopsies, pathologists usually discovered many other diseases besides the one that had carried the person off. Nan was terrified for her mother's sake. She never passed the neighbour's fence without remembering that moment.

Whenever Nan or one of her brothers caught the flu, the mumps, or even something as straightforward as a cold, Mrs. Adams was like Florence Nightingale herself. Everyone said she should have been a nurse. It was her biggest regret, Mrs. Adams often said, that she had not gone into training. Being ill with something ordinary, not threatening, meant missing school, and shining half-moon bedpans, thermometers, a bed to feign sleep in all day; or a thick, warm blanket on the living room couch, eating raisins and squares of cheese and watching sentimental romantic movies with titles like "Song Without End."

There was only one time that Nan could remember—except when she was five and her brother dropped a brick on her head—when she really thought that death was upon her. She had been down the street in a driveway and some of the other girls were skipping double-dutch, and the boys were playing rough at baseball on the lawn. Nan had been on her bike—her first two-wheeler which was too high because originally it had been Mrs. Adams' and was passed down—and she fell from it so hard, the ground met her so violently, that a vast thudding blackness came before her eyes. She could not breathe. All her cries and struggles to escape death were held back by an enormous pressure in her lungs. Her own mother had raced out of the house and down the street wearing her slip and brassiere. Nothing on but that. Breathing again and white-faced and crying, Nan had been carried—by whom? her father?—back home, and looking up she had seen a neighbour watching out his front window, grinning, laughing at the fuss and at her mother's white slip.

Nan dried herself off, carefully daubing at her toe. While she dressed in her housecoat, she decided to make a piece of toast to take to bed with her. She enjoyed eating in bed. Before leaving the bathroom, she bent over to scrutinize the cut. She could have wept at the thought of never walking again, being confined to a wheelchair, dependent perhaps forever on her parents. Never able to get away from anything. Never able to return to the woods where, even if she were thinking about death again, the thought had less power over her.

There was a spot in the woods that she went to, even in winter, where she could be assured of being alone; where the only prints in the snow were those left by rabbits, sometimes by deer. One afternoon, near supper when the sky was wintry slate-grey, she had gone into the glade of fir and spruce trees to sit and think for a while. Everything was white, deep-green and motionless, silent except for the frozen, hollow-sounding wind blowing higher than the tree tops. Nan liked the way the wind roared. She thought that this would be the sound Time might have. Now and then, a wild piece of wind twisted its way through the trees and dashed her face with the spray of snow it was carrying. The unnameable bass power of the wind above the silent clearing made her care less urgently about herself. The voice inside her head stopped and her sense of dread went away for a while.

She went out to the kitchen to make some toast. After a few minutes, she was shaken out of a daydream by the sight of smoke curling up the wall. Behind her, Mrs. Adams, hardly making a sound, had come into the kitchen. Brushing past Nan, she pulled the burning bread from the stuck toaster and, turning, looked from Nan's face to her feet. She spied the swollen toe.

"What have you got there?" She looked Nan straight in the eye—a frightened, creased look around her lips and eyebrows.

"Nothing, I cut my toe: it's nothing."

"Hank, come here and take a look at this," Nan's mother called into the living room. Her voice was trembling.

"It's nothing," Nan repeated dully.

Mr. Adams came with his forehead wrinkled, his mouth tight with hesitation, the newspaper still in one hand. He smiled as he bent over, so much a hopeful, painful smile that Nan nearly broke into tears.

"Just a cut," he said. "You've been in that bathtub so long using up my hot water that the skin's swelled around—but it's just a little cut."

Nan felt tears stinging her throat and eyes. She ducked her head and waited for her parents to allow her to escape. She was safe then. She would not end up like the cousin from Barrie who had had a child's funeral with the old aunts crying into hankies. Nan remembered the shock of seeing the dead boy all waxy and gleaming like a perfect, polished mannequin, abed in the purest ivory satin borders, looking ceramic in his stiff, little boy's suit. The adults had looked hopeless and angry; they had buried their faces into their hands and the deep black coat collars.

"I don't know—you take these things too lightly. Look at that red streak; that's the first sign of gangrene," Mrs. Adams said as she tried to push the toe from side to side.

Nan sucked in her breath and could not let it out. At the point when she thought she would burst and reveal herself, she saw her father smiling easily and suddenly she recalled something. She had once been terrified of him. When she was much younger, she had clutched her mother's legs retreating through the door to a choir practice, and had screamed with terror at being left alone with her father. She had not grown up with him, not really. He had often come home after she was already in bed. She suddenly remembered the look on his face that evening, and they way he had continued to stare at the newspaper in his lap.

"Don't put a bandaid on it, Nan. Let it breathe," he said, winking at her.

"But it's draining—it'll make a mess of the sheets." Nan's mother looked up at him, still holding Nan's toe.

Mr. Adams reached up and scratched the back of his sun-burned neck. "It should breathe."

Nan caught her father's eye quickly and hoped, with a desperate inarticulateness that he would see her relief and gratitude.

"Of course," Mrs. Adams sighed threateningly. "What's another wash tomorrow?" She went to pour herself a coffee from the stove.

In her bedroom, Nan closed the door and took her housecoat off, laying it sideways on the floor against the space between the door and rug. She could not sleep with

15

any light coming in.

The bedroom was a dusky rose at night with two paint-by-numbers of ballerinas above the dresser, a rose rug, and a closet where Nan kept her books and code-written diaries, letters written to secret friends in lemon juice, her first Bible, a map of forts in the woods—an X marking her secluded clearing in the grove of spruce trees. The codes and X's were so cryptic that no one could have interpreted them.

In bed, beneath the reading lamp, Nan studied her toe and hoped that her father was right. Mrs. Adams was filling a kettle for morning. Nan listened to the familiar sounds: the pipes made a deep rumble as her mother ran the tap.

"Did you lock the door?"

Mr. Adams was saying, "I will now."

"There was a time when we didn't have to worry like this," Nan heard her mother say.

With the light out and bedspread drawn to her neck, a peculiar, familiar sensation began to overtake Nan's body. She felt it running across her skin like a wave washing onto a shoreline and she permitted the feeling to consume her. Suddenly, she had the impression of being twenty feet tall; and then, instantly, of being very tiny, and spreading like smooth, melting taffy in all directions. She felt her feet going numb thousands of miles from her head. She was familiar with the feeling—it was part of a dream that she had first experienced while sick once— with some fever years ago. She experienced it often now and not only when she was ill, but at any time. She could virtually will the sensation to begin.

She was moving through the colour and shape of white—sinking into layers of sand, falling down. And each time she slipped, her feet touched sand. As they did, the sand turned to something cold and slicing that might have been razor blades. The instant her feet touched the cold cutting edge, the sensation turned to sand again,

16

then razor, then sand. At the end, she was always something unrecognizable: a funny awful dot with hardly any shape or size or skin. Because she was still awake, the feeling she had now was merely pleasant, scarcely a dream at all. She was awake and clean and she felt miraculously healthy. Safe in bed. Perhaps there was a God and he had heard her and given her one final chance. She decided to remain awake for a while. She thought of her father and how he had rescued her this time. She could think about many things and it would be better than falling into the dizziness and black sleep.

The Best Part of Summer

For Maude, the best part of summer is sitting on the dock at Briar Cottage. Looking into the water, she can see the wooden beams, wrapped in soft green fur and running down to the sand—a universe of water spiders and darting insects. Occasionally, she spies a fish in one of the shadows, hideous with its dazed eyes and speckled skin, but shining like a rainbow.

Maude doesn't swim in the lake. She is afraid that a fish might graze her leg; or worse, her feet might become fatally tangled with the weeds.

Her younger brother, Gerry, likes to swim beneath the dock itself. He brings back stories of rusty tins and broken beer bottles. Maude has to imagine what these things look like. Imagining comes easy—it is something she does all the time. No one in the family can dream the way Maude does.

The sunken beer bottles probably belong to Uncle Larratt. Briar Cottage—like every cottage along this part of the lake—belongs to Maude's uncle, because of an inheritance. "I'd give my eye-teeth to have been left this resort," her mother always says. "If only someone could talk Larratt into lifting a paint brush instead of a bottle for a change."

For a long time, Maude has thought her mother would give her eyes and her teeth to own Briar Cottage.

She imagines her mother trailing across the wide lawn of the lodge or standing sternly like a queen on the main dock, her gums bleeding, dark holes beneath her eyebrows.

It's true that the cottages need a coat of white paint. Still, everyone likes Uncle Larratt. Especially Maude, though he frightens her when she is least expecting it. It's hard to believe that Uncle Larratt and Mother are brother and sister. Maude has noticed people become watchful when her mother enters a room. But Uncle Larratt's arrival anywhere marks the beginning of laughter.

Uncle Larratt spends every day of the summer limping about his property, a smile playing at the corners of his mouth. He's a big man, tall, with arms the size of most people's legs. White brows fringe his blue eyes and his face is blustering and strong.

His voice is one of the deepest Maude has ever heard, the colour of red earth and shaped like a barrel. And when he breaks the silence of the day and bellows across the lawn, pickerel leap out of the lake. Maude doesn't mind the smell of beer on his breath; it is pungent and inviting. But her mother thinks it's a shame to have the Americans notice. The twenty-acre lodge is distinguished because Americans drive up from far away southern states to stay and spend their money.

"So why have a drunk for a proprietor and ruin the whole idea?" Mother asks each summer.

Something in her voice takes the colour out of things. Maude looks at her uncle and wonders how her mother can feel so disgusted.

It's the middle of July and too hot to sit on the wooden planks of the dock. These days, Lovesick Lake lies beneath a silky, wavering heat that presses everything into silence. No one knows what anyone is doing— not like at home where every day is a straight, taut line: Mother in the kitchen, and Father at work, and Gerry in the basement playing with his guns and trains.

Taking her runners off, Maude starts to walk in the direction of the lodge along the dirt road that winds around the lake. The earth underfoot is soft like the chamois cloth her teacher uses to wipe the blackboard. There are bulrushes and fox-gloves on either side, and water-lilies growing out of thick ugly stems just beyond the shore, impossible to reach. Now and then she hears a noise in the forest. She thinks it might be a rattlesnake, an owl surveying her movements, or a hungry mountain lion down from the hills; sometimes, a sly, lethal stranger.

Up at the main lodge where the American guests stay, it's cooler than on the road because a breeze blows in from the water. From a patio chair, Maude can see the lake and observe the guests taking the flagstone steps down to a high stone wall that surrounds the property. The big dock begins at the foot of the steps, blocked the last two summers by a gate that is kept locked because of Stevie, Uncle Larratt and Vicki's new baby.

"Maude, come on over here and keep score for us fellas," Uncle Larratt calls when he sees that she's alone on the patio chair.

She shakes her head no and sits and watches for muskies to jump in the air beyond the gate and main dock; or else she looks at her legs, which are skinny and beginning to grow a layer of fine blond hair. And when Americans emerge from the large white lodge, she studies them, envious of how they must float carelessly from room to room, smoking, drinking, feeling glad to be in such a beautiful place.

"The furniture in that lodge is worth an arm and a leg," Mother often says.

Maude listens and imagines her mother with one arm only, one leg, a one-sided woman wheelchairing at a terrifying speed down the dirt road from Briar Cottage.

"Maude, come on over here," Uncle Larratt calls across the lawn. "Get out of those shadows and into the

22

sun. Keep score for us fellas while we play a game of horseshoes."

Maude feels herself shrinking: is he demanding that she play horseshoes with him? She slouches into the patio chair.

He keeps insisting. "Come on, I don't like to see anyone as pretty as you not enjoying herself."

She is grateful that Uncle Larratt pretends she is pretty. He thinks Maude is a smart cookie too—and tells her so; gives her riddles that can't be solved just to watch her squirm. She enjoys this as well—any attention from Uncle Larratt is worth its cost.

He plays horseshoes for a while each day with some other men who hang about the resort. They have known Uncle Larratt for many summers. The sound of metal clanging in the powdery silt makes the grass quiver and brings up goosebumps on Maude's spine. She likes that feeling. Her skin tingles as though something invisible is in the air or in her mind. This is the way it should be forever and never end: the metal ringing and the yellow dust falling on the grass, the lake beside the lawn, Uncle Larratt so big and funny.

Not everything is perfect at Uncle Larratt's lodge. There are his two older daughters who have been allowed to run wild, as Maude's mother puts it. Maude waits for the day when she might see one of them racing down the road away from the lodge, her arms flailing and her face wild like an animal's. And then there is Uncle Larratt's wife, Vicki—not Aunt Vicki, just Vicki.

"Your Uncle Larratt was a finer person before he married Vicki," Mother often says to Maude. "He didn't drink the way he does now."

The story is engraved on Maude's mind like initials inside a locket. But just in case, she wants to hear it again and let her heart swell at the terrible things possible in a person's life. Her mother is in a good mood when Maude appears interested.

"Larratt was never the same after he had to marry Vicki. The only good thing she ever did was have Stevie when she was practically old enough to get the pension. It's not in your aunt's nature to be helpful at a place like this—she's not what you'd call a real worker."

As far as Maude has observed, Vicki never does anything but work. She is never idle, always cooking, sweeping, scrubbing, hanging clothes out to dry. At the end of the day, she must throw herself down, still dressed, onto the bed to sleep.

There are other stories about her—how at Christmas one year Mother told Vicki she wanted silk underwear from someone, and Vicki passed it on to every possible relative so that Mother got only silk underwear, twenty pairs at least, and not another thing. And that Vicki, when she opens her Christmas present, every year, holds it up and tells the others in the room watching, "I don't know what I'd ever do with a thing like this," no matter what it is.

But Maude doesn't mind Vicki, despite the stories about Christmas and her high-pitched voice and her skin, which is the colour of porridge. There are times when she is quite friendly and reassuring, though you can't be sure she isn't thinking what a pest you are.

So it's a surprise when, on Tuesday night—after the last motorboat has faded into silence—Mother suggests, "Let's walk up to the lodge and see what people are doing up there."

Maude's father stays in Briar Cottage, reading a book by the yellow lamplight.

"You can barely see your hand in front of your face," Mother says, a dark, sturdy figure walking ahead of Maude and Gerry.

Then they are standing in Vicki's kitchen. She is still wearing her day-time cotton dress. She keeps rubbing her forehead and tiny white flakes of skin fall off and float away. When she talks, her mouth clacks. She

24

mentions Uncle Larratt and Maude stiffens. Vicki is shaking her head and looking through the kitchen door. Mother nods and makes a sorrowful sound in the depths of her throat. Maude keeps her face averted as her mother and Vicki go on talking like best friends.

"It's a crying shame," her mother says.

"What sort of example has he ever set for the girls?" Vicki asks. "And what sort of a life is it for me?"

It would be a special treat to see Uncle Larratt. But the house behind Vicki is silent. The baby must be in bed by now. The older sisters are nowhere to be seen.

On the way back to Briar Cottage, Maude asks about Uncle Larratt's absence.

"He's in town getting soused," her mother mutters.

Uncle Larratt must be in the nearby village at this minute, throwing his head back at someone's joke, making everyone laugh with him. Maude wonders whether her own father does that when he leaves the house to go to work—throw his head back and laugh at a remark. For some reason, she and Gerry have not made their father light-hearted and funny.

You can't tell whether Stevie takes after Vicki or Uncle Larratt yet. Mother has pictures of him—blond, smug, toddling carelessly across the lawn. And one of Stevie on Uncle Larratt's knee.

You often see Uncle Larratt with his son like that, his boy on his lap—a bottle in one hand and Stevie steadied with the other. People who stroll across the lawn and say "Isn't he cute?" bewilder Maude. Babies are ugly and helpless. And there is no worse sound in the world than a baby screaming.

At least Stevie has some hair this year. He's only two and roams about the resort being fed tidbits like a puppy. The Americans give him popcorn and chocolate chip cookies and cups of Freshie, which he spills down his terrycloth suit. He is a favourite topic of conversation: a definite shape and sound in Uncle Larratt's voice.

After lunch on Wednesday, when no one is watching, Maude picks Stevie up on the patio chair. She studies his face carefully and he stares back at her in amazement. His eyes are blue like Uncle Larratt's, and his skin is pink. It feels like the soft yellow dust of the lake road or a lily pad warming in the sun when you run your hand across his cheeks and fat little arms.

Maude studies him and thinks about his being Uncle Larratt's. She thinks about how easy it is to dislike someone who is loved just for being himself, just for being alive. She wishes Stevie hadn't been born. Uncle Larratt has been less interested in other things since he got a son, and when people pay attention to Stevie, Maude feels small and uneasy. Someday, the entire resort will be Stevie's.

Stevie becomes restless. Maude is glad to let him down. Away he goes, falling and getting up and going off. Perhaps an hour will go by and you won't be able to find him anywhere, unless he's left a trail of plastic boats and animals behind him. Maude watches him toddle across the lawn and sees Geraldine coming to catch him. Geraldine is the youngest of Uncle Larratt and Vicki's grown-up daughters. It was a surprise to everyone when Stevie came along. Maude doesn't see her girl cousins very often. Marnie has left for Toronto to be a legal secretary—"The only one who's made anything of her life," Maude's mother says; and Geraldine waits on people at the lodge dining room.

They are sullen girls who wear low tops and too much lipstick. Over the years, as one succeeded the next in the dining room, they have done nothing but gripe about living so far from town, away from the dances and the boys. Once last summer, Maude watched as Geraldine lifted Stevie out of his stroller and hit his bottom with a ping-pong paddle. She is cranky and white-skinned like her mother, the last daughter at home, preoccupied, mystifying.

But it's hard to imagine what it would be like having a father whose voice is deeper than the lake and whose breath smells of sweet, strong beer. Something must have made Geraldine so bad-tempered. At breakfast, she sets the plate of bacon and eggs onto the table in front of you and gives it a little shove so that for a minute it looks as if the plate may skid right onto your lap. The dining room is small and if she can bump into your elbow, she will—but she would never do that to an American. Maybe she hopes one of them will turn into an admirer, whisk her away from her father's summer resort and off to Florida forever.

Maude wonders about Uncle Larratt and his daughters and how they don't have anything to do with each other. Maude's father is quieter, more earnest and gentlemanly than Uncle Larratt, who keeps pictures of Jayne Mansfield on his boathouse walls. Maude is very proud and shy of her father. Uncle Larratt, she likes in a different way. He is the overseer of her favourite place in the world: the lord of summer—a fragile week once a year when Maude is finally free and can dream without being interrupted.

* * *

On Thursday, it is overcast. Briar Cottage is a dreary place to be. Maude, Gerry and Father play Cribbage and Scrabble. They eat chips and cheesies, drink orange pop from bottles. Mother is lying down, trying to sleep despite the occasional rumble of thunder. Maude watches through the window and prays for the sun. All day, the cottage feels like a small, unhappy cave.

When the rain stops at suppertime, the sky looks wild. It's hard to tell whether the storm is retreating or gathering force. On the horizon, the sky is black and blue. A shining strip of silver separates it from the lake. A scent of firecrackers lingers about the cabin. Up at the lodge, the guests will be feeling sticky. The crickets chirp cautiously under the dripping ferns. It is dark and quiet.

Gerry and Maude go outside and run through the trees around the cottage, celebrating the night—and the day behind them that they have lived and won't see again. The tension of the long afternoon hangs stiffly over the lake and in the spaces between the pine trees.

Maude realizes she is feeling close to her brother. Sometimes, he is easy to dismay, and it's tempting to be mean with someone who is secretly weak or frightened. For a moment, Maude believes that her existence is faultless after all, linked by things as strong and vast as the earth underfoot, the trees like brave spirits all around. She knows that Gerry is experiencing the same sudden feeling and that she will always, at least, have her brother.

Behind the cottage where the rocks are covered with moist, glistening moss, Maude slips and her knee lands on a nail in a board. With the blood trickling down her leg, she hobbles back to the cabin, pushing Gerry out of the way when, stricken, he tries to stop and help.

Facecloths and dishes of warm water are brought into the living room. Maude's mother and father kneel to examine the injury and Maude's breath is cut short when "the nearest hospital" is mentioned. Till this, her parents' concern has made her feel rare and fussed over. She feels dizzy and ill suddenly. An old joke rings in her ears: "There must have been a mistake at the hospital. Someone must have switched babies. I couldn't have had a child like you."

"What do we have here?" Uncle Larratt's voice booms through the open screen—'awakening the dead', as Mother puts it later. Maude's parents on their knees, and Gerry, pale and silent on the sofa, grieving for a lost moment, look up to see Uncle Larratt standing barefoot on the porch. He is conducting his nightly check on things. His face is beer-red and, in the lamplight, moths and mosquitoes circle above his head like a wild halo.

"She'll be all right, Larratt. She fell on something—a nail or something. It's such a mess at the back of these cottages," Mother says as Uncle Larratt comes through the door. She stands up. Maude looks past her as Uncle Larratt lurches into the room.

"Oh, Larratt," Mother says under her breath.

He winks at Maude and her brother and digs his hand into his pocket, peering down at the wounded knee as he draws out a Lovesick Lake souvenir jackknife. The blade gleams and smells of worms and fish.

He inspects the cut, glancing up at Maude from beneath the jungle of his white eyebrows. After a long silent moment, he leans back: "I do believe this knee will have to come off," he says.

Maude tries to keep from crying. Too late, she sees his teasing, triumphant grin, and she knows that everyone else has caught on and is laughing. Uncle Larratt never says "sorry." Maude's knee is bound in strips from an old bed-sheet and Uncle Larratt sits down for a while in Briar Cottage and accepts a cup of coffee.

"We can't sleep in this heat anyhow," Mother says.

"It's the humidity—like this every July," Father agrees.

The grown-ups sit down to talk. Gerry, anxious to please, spreads the game of Snakes and Ladders on the card table. Maude does not want to play. She is moved by the smarting of the antiseptic cream on her knee, the deepening hour, and by Uncle Larratt's presence in the cabin. She rolls the dice unthinkingly and moves the wrong man.

In a voice that is like a cavern in the moist night air, Uncle Larratt talks on into the evening. The black lake outside the screen is alive, slapping against the rocks. The evening would be perfect, but they are talking about Stevie.

"That one's getting smarter every day," Uncle Larratt pronounces as he waves his cup, letting some drops fall on the table. "Did you hear what he did today? Got into my truck."

"But how could he?" Mother demands.

"He scrambled up the fence and popped onto the front seat."

"How is a two-and-a-half year old going to open the . . ." Mother begins.

"He didn't," Uncle Larratt grins and slaps his knee. "I left the door open. When I got back, the little bugger was on the front seat. Isn't that something?"

Mother shakes her head and lights a cigarette. The smoke curls up to the rafters. "You're careless, Larratt. You keep him fenced in with the stone wall but you've still got to watch him better. There'll be hell to pay if he gets into the guests' rooms."

Father sets his cup down. "I don't think so— Stevie is everybody's pet. They'll take a story back to the States about how Larratt's kid got into their things this year. That's how family legends get started."

"That talk's for women!" Uncle Larratt raps his hand on the table and laughs. "It's a great thing having a son," he says, slowly nodding his head. "You've got someone to leave it all to. If I didn't have a son, I'd just sell the whole damned thing."

"All my family heirlooms go to Gerry because he keeps up the name," Mother says firmly, proudly. "But everything will be split evenly—we keep things even," she adds quickly.

Maude looks up at Gerry. He is engrossed in the game.

* * *

Early in the morning, the storm has dissolved. Taking one of the lifejackets, Maude slips out of the cottage. At the dock, she gets into the old Briar Cottage rowboat, placing her lunch-bag beside her and a fishing rod at her feet.

The water ripples and makes a sucking sound as Maude rows. A voice coming from the cottage makes her stiffen with alarm for a moment. Then, she recognizes it as Mother, saying, "Roll over." The exasperation in her voice carries across the water like an echo. Father's snores are very faint in the distance. When they get out of bed, they will find Maude's note, 'Gone fishing'. Here at the lake, things are easier, freer, than at home.

Maude begins to row again. Many feet from shore, she is still able to see her horse figurines and transistor radio in the window of her room: possessions she brings to Briar Cottage to make it feel like home.

Hatch Bay is a ways off. To get there, Maude must row past the lodge and main dock—and hope that the Americans aren't up yet.

"Where are you off to so early?" one of them might ask as Maude rows past.

"Hatch Bay."

"Where's that? Might make good fishing . . ." they'd say to one another and her secret spot might be taken away—something which must never happen.

She passes the silent dock and rows with renewed vigour. The power boats rise and fall in unison. Her knee stings beneath its bandaids and gauze as she rocks back and forth on the rowboat seat.

It takes twenty minutes to row to Hatch Bay; then she must manoeuvre the boat beneath a bridge. On the other side, the lake floats over land that was once a farmer's field. Here, an immersed jungle sways beneath the boat. Weeds that could be snakes reach toward the surface. Maude rows in circles whenever she spies fish hiding in the wilderness below. They see her and dart away. As she rows, she watches for half-sunken logs, waiting like icebergs to gouge the boat.

31

Imagine draining the marsh—even better, draining the whole lake. People's questions would be answered; mysteries would be solved: the hulls of boats, some that went down in storms, others smashed up by drunken cottagers; fishing rods crisscrossing the lake bed like pick-up sticks; snowmobiles that plunged through the ice in winter; the skeletons of snapping turtles and fish with red and yellow flies snagged in their mouths. Other skeletons.

Maude imagines the dancing, whispering lake dried up. But it will never happen and she is glad of that. Even in school during the winter, the mysteriousness of the lake and the feeling of Uncle Larratt's presence are part of her. To think about him and Briar Cottage is a comfort if something goes wrong or gets frightening during the day, which it sometimes does because Maude dreams.

"If you keep dreaming so much, someday you'll get stuck and never wake up," her mother threatens when stories filter home from Maude's teachers.

A treasured dream is that she, Maude, becomes Uncle Larratt's favourite and that, by some enchanting twist the lodge is left to her.

* * *

She must be asleep. Maude tries to lift her head and knows then that she is having a dream. The sun seems to have cut through her body like something made of metal.

The boat has drifted over to the east side of the marsh. It is after lunch; the sun is behind the trees. Maude sits up. And then she hears it: some sort of commotion, voices calling.

They're searching for me, Maude thinks.

She feels herself shrivel at the possibility that they know where Hatch Bay is—that she has fooled herself into believing they don't. There are many voices, some

32

dangerously near the marsh. Feeling sick, Maude begins to row. Once she has steered the boat through the tunnel onto the open water, she moves more quickly. The smell of firecrackers hangs in the air again, as though lightning has struck or is about to.

At the main dock, Maude ties her boat up. Still dazed from the sun and her dream-filled sleep, she goes through the gate and up the flagstone steps to a circle of adults gathered on the lawn to learn the news: Stevie is missing.

Unnoticed, Maude walks among the guests. She wonders about Stevie and tries to listen to what people are saying. He often trots off like this—but they say he's been gone all morning. Mother is wandering toward the boathouse, her hand cupped to her mouth, and Gerry is trailing behind her. Vicki and Uncle Larratt, their voices separated by the woods and the cottages, call out for their son. Geraldine walks by, not speaking, her eyes squinting in the late afternoon sun. Father must be in the woods behind the lodge.

"Stevie!"

The voices fly out of the woods and get tangled in the slapping noise of the Canadian flag, fluttering in the breeze.

"Stevie!"

Surely he can hear—unless he is really in trouble or has strayed too far. He must have fallen asleep somewhere.

Maude feels the urge to squeal out loud or kick her heels in mid-air and laugh. Different feelings prick at her back. She'll be a hero—a heroine—if she is the one to find him.

He may have wandered down by Briar Cottage—bet no one thought of looking there, or even supposed he could walk that far. Or he may have climbed into a guest's bed in the lodge. The Americans look bewildered, put off maybe that again today a meal is being held

33

up for the sake of the kid: too many things can go wrong in this Ontario wilderness. Maude wants to stick her tongue out at them and say, "Yes, that's right!"

The old men sit in the lawn chairs by the horse-shoe pits, holding their beer bottles but not drinking, and they talk softly—they're too old and short-sighted to help. The American tourists walk carefully around them and don't say "Hello." They walk down to the high fieldstone wall that lines the shore and toward the boat-house, calling, carrying their dripping glasses of liquor.

Maude walks down to the main dock to row back to Briar Cottage. She will eat something, search the cottage for the baby, and then walk along the dirt road to see if he has gotten lost in the bushes. Uncle Larratt will like her even more for this. If only she could be the one to find Stevie. Everyone would feel differently about her.

The large motor-boats whine as they scrape each other's sides, bobbing in the water. As she crouches to untie the rowboat, an uneasiness creeps into Maude's stomach. She stands up and walks to the edge of the dock.

In the smooth black water, her face distorts. Far below her, with the slippery green ferns and rocks, the baby face of Stevie stares up, his eyes unmoving black beads.

Shocked, she stares out over the lake to let the moment wash over her. She doesn't look a second time at her drowned cousin, afraid of the dark roaring pull. Her legs are bending; they are so light she feels she may float in the air, or pitch forward into the blackness with Stevie.

You drowned, she thinks. She trembles with the impulse to laugh out loud in horror.

The calls continue to echo around the grounds. Maude stares over her shoulder at the lodge. Someone has checked the dock too quickly or not at all, she thinks. Afraid to look here. Leaving the worst till the last.

34

They might think she has pushed Stevie off the dock and watched him drown. She wonders if anyone has noticed her yet, hesitating, frozen white on the edge of the water.

A solution takes form in her mind. She could snag his overalls with the fishing rod and drag him back to settle on the jungle floor of Hatch Bay. Otherwise, things will never be the same for Uncle Larratt. She pictures herself rowing back to Hatch Bay, towing the baby's body. Someone might see what she is doing. And Stevie will be too heavy, water-logged.

Maude's legs take her stiffly along the dock and up the flagstone steps. She sits on the patio chair to wait and to hold the secret knowledge a few minutes longer. She watches people pass the patio, guests, Geraldine and Vicki, her own father—his brow contorting the way it has in the past when he's been angry with Maude.

Then Uncle Larratt comes out of the main entrance to the white lodge. His face is red, about to burst—as if his face has had something hurtled at it: a fistful of gravel or scalding liquid. Maude can see the perspiration shining on his forehead and above his mouth. He limps across the lawn, rapidly, stumbling like a blind man toward Vicki whose face turns hard and hateful as she stares at Uncle Larratt and turns her back on him.

Maude ducks her head, embarrassed at having witnessed such a thing. She wonders if Stevie has drowned because of Uncle Larratt's big, easy-going happiness. She has been the first one to see the baby in the lake—she is sure of that. It will take some time for Uncle Larratt to get over this, but when he does, Maude will be his favourite.

"I'm ahead of them," Maude realizes. She glances up as Uncle Larratt and Vicki gaze at the dock, the unlocked accordion-style gate. A hush settles over the grounds. It is a strange sensation knowing what is about to happen to people.

35

At the last moment, Uncle Larratt seems to notice Maude sitting alone on the patio, but immediately he is distracted. He looks at her face without expression; his eyes slip away. He doesn't see Maude lift her arm to point her finger toward the dock. She is invisible, someone else's child, someone to tease perhaps.

More people stop to stare down the flagstone steps to the open gate and the long dock where the boats are bobbing. Maude can't see the looks on their faces. She can hear people's voices, "Oh, God", or maybe it's just the breeze rustling through the leaves that are baked dry in the summer heat.

She gets up to walk back to Briar Cottage. The shadows of branches and the long arms of trees move on the dirt road like lacy curtains. She feels herself moving away from everyone else, their voices rising in the distance stretching behind her. There is a long afternoon ahead of her and no one knows where anyone is.

Well Beaten Paths

The sun fell forever through the cedars all around. Where the light landed in the creek, the water was pale gold but where it curved about the bank, it was shimmering green. Alex spied a fish, a long, brownish green shape, basking in the deep pool where the water stopped rushing momentarily. She and Wanda put down their sandwiches and crawled to the edge of the bank to look.

"It's a trout or a salmon," Alex whispered.

"No, it's an ordinary smelt," Wanda scoffed.

The fish twitched and vanished.

"It was too coloured to be a smelt," Alex insisted.

She stood up and returned to her lunch which was laid out on the grass. She wasn't sure at all how one fish differed from another. But it was important to pretend in the face of so many mysteries. They each had cucumber and lettuce sandwiches and interesting things to nibble on throughout the long, hot day—pickles, raisins, an apple, peanut butter cookies. Wanda's cookies were store-bought because her mother worked. Her mother did not get along with her father. Somehow, these details about Wanda's mother were connected and gave the other mothers something to talk about.

It was noon hour and they were languid. Since early morning, when they had slipped from their sleeping homes, they had been traversing many paths, assuring themselves of the constancy of the woods and adding to their sense of its geography. Because they always did, they had checked the fox den on the side of Tower Hill, and then the deserted Boy Scout camp of Farm Slope just to know that nothing had disturbed its overgrown and dormant condition. Along the paths, they had resolutely pulled out small wooden stakes, each one waving with a plastic orange flag. They would do whatever was necessary to block the city's development of their woods. They worked at this task without feeling frantic or deliberate, and took the stakes back to their fort to use as firewood.

The two of them knew the woods very well. Alex knew it better, since she sometimes came on her own, although a solitary jaunt would often leave her feeling guilty. The woods were something she knew were shared with Wanda. But she was drawn to them more. Wanda was one to get nervous and stay home for the three hours between school and darkness in order to study for tests. So Alex often went alone.

They both had dogs. Wanda's father, a large man, distant and sometimes sullen, had bought two hounds for his fall hunting trips. Alex's dog properly belonged to her older brother but there was no argument that she had taken over in terms of both training and loyalty. Spike could now "Heel, Come and Stay," but he had never learned to shake a paw. He was only a mongrel.

They had ideas for making money.

"We should start a day nursery and have finger painting and singing afternoons," Alex said.

They were walking home now, slowly, taking the time to stop and watch the pheasants as they rose startled and swift out of the overgrown and tangled bushes. They counted on their fingers the children under five who lived in the neighbourhood and would be free in summertime to attend such a nursery in Alex's backyard.

Then it was a neighbourhood newspaper they wanted to edit. They counted on their fingers the articles—social events and certain details about different families—they would have to include.

"How about a Dear Alex column?" Alex suggested. She bit into a toasted cornmeal muffin. Wanda's mother rolled her eyes and popped two more flat muffins into the toaster. Alex watched her moving at the kitchen sink. She liked Wanda's mother very much, although it embarrassed her to know that these feelings were visible and considered unnatural. But everything about her was better than ordinary—her blondness, her posture at the steering wheel of the station wagon as she drove past Alex's house to work every morning, her rushed, knowing voice—even the butter that dripped warm and golden from the muffin was better. Even her briskness was something that Alex found wonderful, though that frightened her as well. Once, Wanda's mother had stood with her hands on her hips in the upstairs bedroom and laughed with sparkling, derisive eyes at Alex because her underwear could be seen through her thin cotton shorts. She was like that: welcoming one day and inhospitable, even mean, the next.

Now she crossed the kitchen and laid her hands on the table where Wanda and Alex were dotting up crumbs of cornmeal with their fingertips. She was tall and blonde and gaunt.

"Dear Alex," she began wryly. "I have a husband who leaves me for weeks on end to hunt and who has now brought two dirty, smelly, noisy hounds into my basement where they regularly do their business on the floor. What should I do?" She stood and waited, bemused, tapping her purple fingernails on the top of the chair. She had the "fed-up" look on her face.

Alex considered. "Dear reader," she began, "your only solution is to get a new basement."

Wanda hooted and clapped her hands and pushed her chair back from the table to stare triumphantly at her mother who had to laugh too. Wanda loved to feel

40

victorious. It was a wonder to Alex why Wanda did not support her mother in the battle between her parents. It was beyond her, and always she felt an affinity with Wanda's mother, as if something crucial lay within her power—crucial because it had to do with Alex.

The day was windy and blue. The main path wound around the trees and alongside the marsh before disappearing vaguely at the base of Tower Hill. They had left the moist and tangled marsh largely unexplored. This part of the woods, mostly bog, was always darker than even the most deep green and shaded sitting areas among the cedar trees, almost as if the sun deliberately overlooked the marsh; or the damp, soggy ground absorbed the sun and never released it. Even on this day, when the wind was tossing the trees so wildly that Alex was filled with an increasingly familiar restlessness, the marsh which ran at the end of the field remained dark and still.

The countryside was vivid and moving with autumn. The fragrance of apple orchards to the north blew across the field as Wanda and Alex walked, mostly silent, and they could see apples—crimson dots—on the trees in the distance.

They avoided the marsh. The boys were sometimes there. You could recognize their voices—the same boys that Wanda and Alex had grown up with, and played hockey with for one winter after another on neighbourhood rinks, boys they easily defeated when it came to the hierarchy of first, second and third in class. But who had suddenly taken on a new separateness. It would have been terrible to meet them in the woods. Terribly wrong. It was infuriating enough to even hear their voices in the distance. To see anyone else in the woods was disturbing. Someone might change part of it.

Alex liked to think that by pulling out the foot-long, flagged stakes, she was thwarting powers at large, that she was managing single-handedly to hold something inevitable at bay. There was no one else she wanted to share her world with, though there were times when she imagined bringing Wanda's mother into it so that she, too, would revel in the trees. She liked to think of Wanda's mother walking beneath the same trees with the wind rearranging her yellow hair. But this was merely a dream because it had somehow been made clear that Wanda's mother had long ago turned her back on such possibilities. One Saturday morning nearly a year before, an ambulance, very tentatively—as if it knew that it did not belong in this neighbourhood and wanted to turn back—had pulled into Wanda's driveway and five minutes later Wanda's mother was carried out on a stretcher. Nothing but a bulky, red blanketed shape. Ever since that morning a year ago, Alex had often thought how she would like to invite Wanda's mother along.

This particular afternoon was cool. From the marsh, four of the boys from school suddenly caught sight of Wanda and Alex on top of Tower Hill with the dogs at their heels. With a loud cheer, they gave chase across the field and paths that led to the Hill. Wanda and Alex looked at each other and laughed. They could do that—take just enough time to look at each other before turning to race along a lesser-known path towards the thicker part of the woods where they would be assured of outsmarting the boys.

As she ran, Alex felt afraid and exhilarated. She never for an instant dreamed that the boys would catch her; and even if they did, what would they dare? They lived on the same street as she did! But something terrible might be said and she was fearful because they were in a group, and boys changed in larger numbers. Her knowledge of the woods would save her. Her closeness to it would protect her and invest her with power more than the proximity of one home to another in the neighbourhood would.

42

Exhausted, and smothering their roars into the bed of moss and branches which made up their Northern Fort, Wanda and Alex caught each other's eye and grinned. There was, of course, the undeniable possibility that their fort would not be the camouflaged stronghold they imagined. But they refused to admit that fear out loud.

"By the time they get to the top of Tower Hill, they'll be so pooped, they'll give up," Wanda said in a superior way.

"Whisper!" Alex demanded excitedly. But she laughed widely and noiselessly. "They don't know the paths the way we do!" she said confidently.

Wanda nodded. But then she was thoughtful and her grey freckled eyes were cast down as she remained inside an uncommunicated moment.

"What would they do if they caught us?" she asked, looking up at Alex.

Alex shrugged and leaned back on the moss and branches.

"Remember what they did to that girl in Grade 8? Peggy Lynd?"

Alex nodded uncomfortably. The very name was like a wicked magic spell. The boys—older ones—had taken that girl into the woods, and undressed her. The next day they had stolen chalk from the classroom and written about it all over the sidewalks which led to and from the school that everyone attended: "Peggy stripped."

There was something awful and weakening in sharing someone's shame.

"She must have let them do it—there's a difference," Wanda said.

The woods around them remained silent for a long time so they knew that the boys had given up.

Sometimes they went downtown on Saturdays and looked at the magazine racks. Some of the magazines at the far

43

end of the rack depicted women—nude women and strippers—being tortured by large muscular men. The illustrations always made it look as if the story were happening during a time of war. One showed a soldier holding a woman's head beneath a tub of water and preparing to shoot in order to deafen her. They knew what the gun's explosion under water would do to the woman because Wanda's father had explained it to them. He had magazines much like the ones they saw on Saturdays. In a matter-of-fact tone of voice, he described how such a thing would create a concussion in the woman's head. Wanda's mother was ironing by the kitchen sink. "Why do you want to know about that sort of thing?" she said, looking as if she had eaten something which had gone bad. She looked at Wanda and Alex with great suspicion. She did not look at Wanda's father.

They were walking the dogs across the wide fallow field that skirted the woods. Wanda was ill. She had a headache or a stomach cramp. Her hand kept fretting from her forehead to her abdomen. Alex couldn't be sure.

"Want me to take them?" she offered.

Wanda dumbly unwound the leashes of her hounds from either wrist and Alex strapped them to her own. Spike was free to gallop as he pleased but the hounds were purebred and had to be restrained. They had only recently learned to shake a paw.

Half-way across the field, a rabbit zigzagged across their path.

"Hold them!" Wanda cried.

Alex tried feverishly to unwrap the two leashes from her wrists. A second later she was on her stomach and being dragged by the hounds across the hard-ridged land. Her face took in the deep rich scent of winter until her nose struck a hard bump in the land. Then she couldn't smell anything or hear anything. When the dogs finally tangled in barbed wire twenty feet off, Alex was tangled too. Blood streamed down in alarming pulsating gushes from her nose. She lay on the ground while the dogs panted beside her, unhurt, and while Wanda ran up, she felt her face. Her nose, from the inside, felt perfectly flattened. She experienced mild surprise when her fingers touched its normal, protruding contours. And she felt that she was blind.

The barbed wire had caught her sideways on the forehead—a swift, painless gash to somewhere around her eye. The world was black with blood. But she knew, sitting up and then slowly standing dizzily, that Wanda was only terrified for the dogs. She looked almost ashamed to see Alex injured. It was a side of Wanda that Alex had always sensed but dreaded to see. Alex walked home the fast way clutching her jacket to her forehead while Wanda took the dogs through the park to her own home.

The scar—the barbed wired had only seared the flesh in a three-inch jagged line from the temple to her left eyebrow—healed quickly. There were jokes about Frankenstein at school.

Alex was afraid for Wanda's mother to see her looking so terrible. She went over one morning. Wanda was in the bathroom, downstairs. Her father had removed the door knob and anybody who wanted could have looked inside.

"Wait for me upstairs in my room," Wanda said.

Alex climbed the stairs and at the landing turned to enter Wanda's bedroom. A funny weak sensation came over her as something out of the corner of her eye caught her attention. Turning her head, she looked down the corridor to the spare bedroom. Wanda's mother was sitting, cross-legged, on the floor. She was building a small fire on the rug, of clothes-pegs and twigs, and was gazing at the flame. She did not hear or notice Alex.

More often now that winter had settled in and Wanda was taking ballet lessons on a different night than Alex, and because she was increasingly unnerved by tests and surprise exams, Alex took to going to the woods alone. Spike went with her and he, in his silent, approving, enthusiastic way, supplied Alex with all the company she needed. It reassured her to hear that Spike was watching and following her as she ran, but taking the liberty of making private forays into the bush. It was during one of these private, cloudy visits to the woods, when she was searching out the paths mantled with snow and following the various tracks left by deer and rabbits, that a singular and strangely familiar feeling came over Alex.

She was sitting on top of Tower Hill and the fields below were yellow and white with dead summer grass and snow; and the public school was a small square fortress in the distance. She felt something change—as if a room in her mind had suddenly opened up. She had a sudden sense of herself as a single figure on top of the big hill, alone as always, and the sense was not a fleeting one as it sometimes was. It was not there and gone but remained in her heart and very much in her stomach, and she knew, with despair, how alone she was. Not because she wasn't with Wanda, though if her friend had been present she might not have been so overcome. But because she was alone. It was the proper and helpless state of being. The wind was dark the way it blew so freezing cold, blowing in even deeper winter from Lake Ontario and across the fields right up the snowy side of Tower Hill through Alex's ski jacket.

Her breasts felt warm. She had her first brassière now—a soft and loving stretch of fabric which felt important against her skin. She felt large and isolated all of a sudden as the silence of the woods grew louder.

She stood up and began to run, floundering through the snow, across a field and into the dark stillness beneath the trees.

She had to slow down here. Many of the trees had fallen and created a precarious latticework of trunks and branches. She crossed these and picked her way through the woods till she came to a thin but sturdy sapling where a year earlier she and Wanda had carved their initials and the date: May 1957. She took her mittens off and ran her white fingers over the scar in the bark.

It was nearly June and the last year of public school. The woods were overgrown and sweet-smelling. Alex picked wild flowers along the path and carried them until the whole huge bunch of unnamed blooms were like thick sap in her hand, melted by the warmth of her palm.

Wanda had found a pointed stick and was forging a path through the bushes alongside the creek, thrashing at the underbrush that scratched at her bare legs. She found a willow branch and stripped it to fashion a kind of whip and discarded the pointed stick in favour of making the willow whistle through the sunny hot air around her.

The path was well-beaten. In a small moment of clearing, in the midst of a group of fir trees, they came upon the charred remains of a small campfire. Cigarette butts were scattered about its edges. Boys had come here to smoke. On top of the burned twigs and ashes, Alex and Wanda discovered a few singed pages from a paperback. The words were faded and yellow with weather and the heat of the fire. But one page was still clear. They held it, one on each side of the page, and read the words to themselves:

> ...fought the woman to the ground. Then they held her, two at her arms, one each at her legs, holding them apart. Then they took turns...

The boys had left this here—how had they come to do that? Had they sat in a circle, smoking, reading this out loud?

"Where's the rest of the book?" Alex said.

Wanda made no response and ran the top of her shoe through the ashes. She looked distant and kept her eyes lowered. For a few minutes, they sought beneath the surrounding underbrush for the rest of the book. Then, silently, Wanda folded the page four times to slip into her shirt pocket. Alex longed to ask here why she was saving it. But she could not find her voice.

The woods were becoming less of a kingdom. It was beginning to be a free-for-all. When Alex was seated at her desk in the school classroom and looked out the window to the east where the woods stretched densely across the meridian, she sometimes saw small coloured specks moving—the jackets of strangers in the trees, and other times, the yellow jacket of city workers. Seeing them there filled her with terrible apprehension. She felt desperate. The clock above the blackboard clicked at each minute. She stared at the classroom picture of Queen Elizabeth in her turquoise satin gown and at the folded ivory fan in her hand.

She was interested in some of the boys. It amazed her to discover that they liked her back—they teased her and one of the boys once pulled her bra strap from behind; at recess when all the Grade 8's were at play, they cried, "Rover, Red Rover, let Alex come over." Wanda was intense and frightened. Her mother was home from the hospital and working again. The mothers who gathered for coffee now and then in Alex's kitchen talked about it. One of them said, loud enough for Alex in her bedroom to overhear, that He drank. He had assaulted Wanda's mother. Alex knew what the word meant butfor a long time she wondered what must have taken place between Wanda's parents.

Their weekends were altered. They made a structure of the day.

"First, we'll go to see our initials and then we'll wait by Tower Hill to see whether the fox has had her litter," Alex planned.

Wanda nodded agreement. We're only pretending to be friends, Alex thought. She didn't know how it had happened. They were both apprehensive.

Earlier they had recognized three boys from a distance gathering in a clearing, observing something that lay at their feet. Later in the afternoon, along one of the central paths, they came upon a rabbit, flies whizzing above its grey and blood massed organs. The rabbit's belly had been flipped open with a knife and a dark patch in the earth had formed a circle around the dead animal.

Trembling, Wanda and Alex quickly moved away. They arrived at their bank by the curve in the creek, and neither felt like eating their sandwiches. The smelt was basking in the sun but they only sat and watched it sleeping.

They were afraid to leave their shelter since they knew that the boys were in the woods as well—they had killed the rabbit and treated it grotesquely. Had they really grown up together?

"I wonder where's the man I'm going to marry?" Wanda said out of nowhere in a dreamy voice.

Alex looked up and away, startled. She shrugged her shoulders. "Somewhere." She felt incomprehensible horror. She felt afraid for Wanda.

"I wonder what he's doing right now," Wanda said. She had a long, wide blade of grass in her fingers that she was splitting into hair width strips.

"Out killing rabbits," Alex wanted to say. But she said nothing, knowing that this time Wanda would not laugh.

They leaned back and looked at the pines shooting up and up to the egg-blue shell of the sky. The dogs were in the underbrush.

"I don't want to ever stop coming here," Alex said.

"Do you think we'll still be coming here when we're old?" Wanda said dreamily.

Alex thought about that. "If I don't I won't be the same as who I am." It didn't make any sense out loud. The sense she had known on Tower Hill a long time ago was still very much with her. But it was something in her that she both hated and loved and wanted to protect. As long as she could know that sense.....

"What do you think of Robert Johnson?" Wanda asked.

Alex laughed and made a scornful face.

"He likes you," Wanda insisted.

They left for school a half hour earlier than was necessary because Robert was a senior safety patrol two blocks away at 8:30 in the morning. He was bossy and superior and laughed as if he had heard about his secret admirers.

Wanda's mother laughed at them, too. "You've got so much time. Don't rush it, for God's sake. You'll be there soon enough."

Alex went to Wanda's house in the morning and ate toasted cornmeal muffins at the kitchen table while Wanda got dressed upstairs. She didn't want Alex to see her dressing. "I like this closet door because you can change behind it," she had said on a different morning, looking around the corner of the door at Alex sitting on the edge of the bed. Alex had smiled helpfully but inside she felt ashamed for Wanda. Some of the girls at the school were wearing lipstick and teasing their hair and nearly everyone had gotten her period. They passed notes between them about the "Red River."

So Alex was left downstairs at the kitchen table. Wanda's mother talked about her work. She was often very excited and her eyes were bright and high. Her face was bruised this morning. She described how she had fallen off a foot-stool and struck the edge of a coffee-table while cleaning. She had been dusting the antlers of a deer's head which Wanda's father had mounted above the make-believe fireplace in the living room. She never referred to the fire.

Many of the girls at school held Wanda and Alex apart because of their dogs and their reputed weekends spent in the woods. It was almost enough to make them not want to go to the woods.

In class, Wanda was silent with despair and intimidation. Alex often got into trouble now because she was loud and laughing, accepting notes from Robert and one other boy. The teachers admonished her—but rarely, because she stood first in the class. She looked at the woods through the classroom window and felt safe.

Alex felt moody. She thought about herself and decided that the storm moving in was affecting her. The sky was scuttling overhead and a layered darkness had descended over the woods. It was August and the heat was intense. She hoped desperately that it would rain. The moisture on the leaves always pulled up the fresh smell of dirt and grasses. She hoped almost feverishly that it would thunder, that the sky would be torn open by a bolt of lightning. She wanted it to strike something only a foot away and fill her heart with terror.

Wanda was silent; she walked alongside and looked in the direction away from Alex. Her mother was threatening to leave her father. There had been yet another ambulance there a week before. "She's sick again," Wanda explained coldly. She was furious.

Somehow they were separated. Alex deliberately, and cruelly she thought, made no attempt to find her friend. She slipped away and fled along a path that she was certain Wanda did not know.

She was torn. Everything was tearing her.

It began to rain.

Loud plopping sounds hit the leaves above her head. Alex sat very still, trembling violently every few moments. No one could see her. Even Spike couldn't find her and she found herself unable to call to him when his scurrying paws rustled in the grass nearby. It was as if the world—the woods and the sky and her body, too—had contracted to isolate her. The very air felt close and threatening.

Some rain drops found their way beneath the bower of leaves. Her head was damp. Then she felt a dampness in her pants. Touching her jeans, she felt a warm wet patch that came up red on her fingers. She stared at it, shocked and frightened.

She had to move. She could not wait here in the bushes forever. Calling to the dog, Alex stood up though she was as drained and grey as the sky overhead. She began to pick her way across the tangled floor of fallen branches and stumps. In the distance, the thin blue sound of a siren rose and then receded.

At a point where the bushes separated slightly, she stood and looked across the field. As if from a long way off, she saw Wanda walking towards home with the hounds around her legs. Alex felt remote and very cut off, and there was something wonderful in the newness and the secrecy of the feeling. She could stand here, knowing Wanda's loss, and let her walk homeward alone, without calling.

When there was no one in sight, she began the long walk home herself.

Left To Be Desired

Every time Claire arrived at the farm, Jackson somehow knew it. If she came across the field, he saw her from one of his windows. Some days, she took a path through the woods so that the barn lay between her and his house as she approached— but that was a long way around, and even then, Jackson often spied her in the barnyard.

Today, she was walking along the road that ran past Jackson's farm. The long grass in the ditch was coated with dust, and the smell of wild raspberries lifted out of the scorched tangle of bushes. Claire climbed Jackson's fence and leapt to the ground, leaving the gate wobbling. She kept her head averted, half-expecting that he might not recognize her, but already she could feel him watching from the house.

Maybe I should go through the barn so he can't see me, she thought. She looked up at the structure glooming darkly ahead of her. Pieces of wood were missing in the roof, and the gaping holes allowed crows and pigeons to fly inside. Hornets' nests the size of spinning tops hung from corners. Maybe abandoned, maybe not. There was a waterlogged smell to the wood, even in the hottest weather—something dank, fetid and unhealthy.

The large door was ajar. Claire went up to it and peered inside. Bales of hay stacked against one wall had softened into the shapes of frozen bison, trailing wisps like stringy hair over the treacherous straw-covered floor. Sometimes, in the middle of the night when she was awake and thinking about things, Claire imagined falling through a rotten floorboard to the stalls on the floor below, lying for hours before being discovered. Or Jackson knowing she was in trouble but not calling for help.

One morning, when she had been kicking through the straw, hoping to find old *Saturday Evening Post* magazines, or a cast-off box of some sort, or pieces of coloured glass, she had instead found a cow's head, the horns still intact, all skin long since gone. She thought about that cow's head a great deal and tried to imagine what had taken place: Why would Jackson cut off a cow's head? Why had he left the head in the straw?

Claire breathed in the deep pungent air of the barn—the smell of oats and soil, of life bursting, of mysteries and secrets in the dark cobwebbed corners. Pulling away, she unlatched the barnyard gate and gazed across the fields, straining to see Blackie. She searched till her eyes were sore, wanting there to be movement, a black shape grazing in the distance. A familiar yearning trembled in her stomach as she realized the pony was still confined to his stall. She glanced about for Ted's car. So he had not yet arrived.

In the barn yard, Claire could hear the pigs shuffling against the trough. Within the sty, the sow was beginning to make bleating noises. At the sound of footsteps, Claire whirled and saw Jackson limping down the narrow path from the house, his jaw working at a wad of tobacco. His German shepherd zigzagged at his feet. The farmer didn't look up, but Claire knew he had seen her. His face was flushed with self- righteousness, a furious anticipation.

She forced herself to walk naturally into the lower barn. She glanced into the annex, a separate part of the barn where Ted boarded his carriage horse, Jewel. Her stall was a warmer, fuller place than those in the lower barn. Ted kept it brimming with uncracked yellow straw. The aroma of new leather, expensive brushes, leathery oils and molasses mixed with oats filtered out of the annex door.

He'll be here tonight, Claire thought. She always knew when to expect him. They were alike where animals and the countryside were concerned. She had been feeling better lately, knowing every evening that Ted might show up. It was no longer just Jackson and herself. And her parents were not as leery about her visits to the farm since Ted, who went to the same church and lived only two blocks away, had moved his horse in.

Some days she walked past his two-storey red brick house hoping to see him or hoping that he would look out a window suddenly and see her. Not call to her across the lawn and force her to speak, exhaust her with the effort of appearing mature and impressive—just see her and maybe think about her for a while. Hopefully, he would come to the farm alone tonight. Not with his two daughters who were much younger than Claire—"the giggle sisters"—or with his wife who was large and pregnant right now—a fact which embarrassed Claire and made her realize how separate from Ted she really was. Ted's wife was always remote behind her dark-rimmed, thick glasses, a mother who uttered vacant pleasantries, unlike Claire's mother who was well known for her blunt, challenging observations. Claire liked being with Ted when he was alone and she could cast appraising glances in his direction, stand beside him and listen to his smooth, measured voice.

"Blackie," Claire said, so he would hear her voice and whinny a greeting. "It's cool in here."

The cobwebs from the roof wafted slightly above her head. The air felt cool and wet. Claire clicked her tongue and reached into her pocket. She stopped abruptly. The black pony was pivoting frantically, lowering his haunches to kick. He flicked his ears and strained on the rope to turn and observe Claire, his enormous brown eyes shining out of the dark.

"Aren't you glad to see me?" she said wonderingly. Why didn't the animal know her voice? Only two days had gone by. It discouraged her to think that Blackie didn't have the intelligence, the instinct, to remember her.

He was tied by a brief rope to his stall—a cement slab elevated above a narrow drain that ran around the barn floor. His haunches relaxed and he whinnied lowly. Claire came forward and stroked his forehead as she brought her hand to his velvet black mouth. The sugar cubes she had brought from home disappeared with one flap of his large lips. His buckets were empty. A bit of straw-flecked water jiggled in one when she prodded it. He did know who she was—of course he did. He nuzzled her arm now and made flapping motions with his lips as though he were trying to bite her forearm.

"You must be thirsty," she said out loud.

She took his bucket to the tap and filled it. She felt what surely missionaries and nurses must feel when they cared for someone, nurtured them back to health and contentment. It must surely be what God felt as he moulded things and watched them grow despite terrible obstacles.

Claire remembered the first time she had spotted the pony two years ago. She had been in the woods and had climbed a hill that overlooked her public school on the edge of town, its dreaded baseball diamond and playing fields, the two new portables, the teachers' parking lot. She had let her eyes slide over to Jackson's farm and sucked in her breath, scarcely able to believe that she was looking at a pony. She had run through the woods and across the fields to Jackson's farm, afraid that by the time she arrived, the vision would have disappeared, or the living pony would have been swiftly removed.

"Your mother know you're here today?" Jackson said behind her.

He was standing in the doorway.

"She doesn't mind my coming." Claire ducked her head so he wouldn't see she was lying. She felt him waiting for her to look at him, keep the conversation going.

Why can't you see what this is doing to Blackie, she thought, keeping him penned up every day for weeks.

At first, it had nearly driven her wild to think of the strain it must be creating on his legs to forever stand tied like this. Then she had read that a horse's knees locked. They could even sleep standing up.

"I don't see why you're so fit to be tied over that horse," Claire's mother had said once.

Fit to be tied, Claire had thought. Nothing was fit to be tied.

She picked up a brush and began to groom the pony. The dust flew up from his back. No matter how hard she pressed into his flanks, the dust continued to rise.

Jackson shuffled by the barn door, several feet away. The red web of veins across his nose and cheeks was deeper, more purple than usual. He was pretending to be busy with a piece of leather and a torn burlap sack in his hands. He slashed the length of leather at the dog's neck, making the animal back away, tail between its legs. Claire felt a familiar apprehension filling her, making her slightly dizzy. It made her uncomfortable when she knew Jackson was observing her.

"Are you going to let Blackie out today?" Claire said, still not looking at Jackson. She held her breath, already knowing his answer. When you wanted something too hard, too desperately, it couldn't happen.

"Can't do it, little girl. Cows are in the field."

"He won't bother the cows; he doesn't when I'm

with him," she pleaded.

"He'll chase them. Bites their teats and then they don't give milk."

Claire flushed. "I'll put a rope on his halter, just in the barnyard. Where is his halter?" she said, looking about, hoping to divert the farmer by drawing him into a search.

"Not when the cows are out."

I could just let you go, she thought. She swallowed painfully to keep from crying. She kept brushing till her hands were aching and made herself think of something else—of sitting in the field with devil's paintbrush and purple clover on the ground and apples overhead and the fields blowing different shades of yellow and gold and green in the breeze, while Blackie grazed and she sketched him. And of riding bareback and leaning backwards to lie on his back and to see the infinite opaque blue sky from that angle.

I could just let you go, she repeated silently.

The last time Jackson had freed the horse, Claire had ridden Blackie while he grazed in the far pasture. Looking up, she had seen a male figure coming through the fields. At first she had thought it was Ted, and her heart had started to pound with excitement. It had been her father. The instant she realized her mistake, she slipped off Blackie's back and leaned against his flanks in the dismal hope that she could convince her father she had been merely leaning all along.

"I thought we told you not to ride the pony when you're alone," her father had said when he was close enough.

She had felt shocked that he would do this: walk a mile up the road to inspect her separate world, check up on her. "I wasn't."

"Oh yes you were," her father had said, but he said it with enough of a smile, which surprised her.

He was often angry at Claire for ruining things.

She disliked doing things with her family such as singing, watching "Sky King" or "Rawhide" on TV, going for drives. Her father had threatened to take her bedroom door off its hinges if she did not join the family. One night, she was in bed crying— already she could not recall why—and he burst into her room, a lunging dark shape in the doorway, and spanked her for making such a raucous. She stopped crying then, too frightened to go on. She felt terribly ashamed for him and for herself now. She did not like him to speak to her alone or to touch her.

They had walked home together, Claire reluctantly. She didn't want to leave the pony so early and she felt odd walking alongside her father.

"What does your mother think of you spending all summer at my place?" Jackson wheezed from the doorway. "Not the thing for little girls to be doing." His words sounded cut in half, breathless.

"I'm not so little. I'm in grade 8 next year," Claire told him. "The summer's going and Blackie's hardly been out. His legs will seize up." This time, she looked straight at the farmer. He looked like an old man, although he was not much older than Ted.

Jackson snorted and spit into the ground. Claire turned away from the discoloured phlegm as it disappeared into the straw.

Her mother said Jackson was queer, locked up alone in his house with no furniture, no paintings, hardly a dish to eat off. Filthy as well. Men were when they lived alone. Her mother said that Jackson had loved a woman once, someone who married another man—one of the worst things that could happen to a person. And Jackson had never married; in a very real sense, therefore, he was a man who had no home. No one respected or liked him.

The dust spraying up from Blackie's neck was making Claire feel sick. His mane was so tangled that the brush would barely penetrate the strands. How does he get it this tangled when he stands in the stall all day? she wondered.

"And your mother doesn't mind you coming around, eh?"

Claire shook her head and pressed the brush vigorously into the pony's flanks. "I wish they'd buy Blackie from you, but they can't afford to."

"Bought that damned fool animal for my nephew and he never rides it. Got bucked off once and that was it," Jackson muttered. "A damned waste of money."

"No one can ride you but me," Claire whispered into the pony's ear.

She put her arm around the horse's neck and breathed in his smell. When he was out in the pasture, he allowed her to pirouette on his back and run from behind and vault onto him. There was no greater pleasure than sitting astride a horse and feeling the warmth and breath ripple through his body. She had never felt such a connection to a living, breathing being before. Getting on him in the barn was awkward, although she sometimes slid onto his back and leaned over to wrap her arms around his neck. The idea of grazing the dark, rotting roof above terrified her. The cobwebs were thick as fishing nets.

She stopped brushing as the bull on the other side of the barn shrieked and shook the chain than ran through its nostrils. Claire stared at the roof overhead, vibrating. The bull kicked at the slats of his stall and there was a splintering noise.

"Do you think that bull could get loose?" Claire said.

Blackie's ears were flat and alarmed.

"Not unless I want him to."

"You've had him tied so long, he's gone crazy," she said accusingly.

Jackson grunted and went out of the barn.

For a few minutes, Claire thought about leaving the farm to avoid the farmer and to take her mind off

Blackie's confinement. She stared at the cement floor thinking of what she might do if she left the farm. But there was no place she would rather be. She continued to work at the pony's coat, polishing it, and stroking his mane and face while she spun miracles, favourite dreams about a new stall for him, better lighting, an English saddle of the palest tan leather. And music. She had read about people piping carols into their horse's stall at Christmas. And that bull—she'd get him out of here. Some people and animals it was better to put out of their misery. Over the top of the stalls, the gleam of the bull's eye caught her own. She looked away from the mad yellow light in its eyes.

She glanced down at the pony's belly. In the shadow of the stall, she saw the animal's cock enormously distended. She had seen it once before when she was brushing him, grooming him until his coat shone and the dust no longer seemed to be lying in layers to his very hide. She stared at it now. It looked rough, as if the skin were partly made of fish scales. She reached the brush forward to test one of the scaly flaps of skin. The horse quivered and struggled to turn his head on the foot-long rope. He was trying to look at her.

She felt strangely uncomfortable suddenly—she didn't like feeling ill at ease around the pony. He was part of her, more than her pet, a kind of sibling, a relative. She didn't like the sense of oddness that had come over her. She had a sudden image of her father passing at the foot of her bed—his bed. For some reason—she had been very young—she had been put into his bed to sleep. He had walked past the foot of the bed without pyjamas on and Claire had lifted her head. The moment had been fleeting and surreptitious.

She went outside and crossed the yard, skirting the large pond. Inside the pig sty, the sow was making human sounds. Two nights earlier, Ted had said the sow was about to give birth. The sounds coming from the low enclosure were frightening, yet Claire remained at the fence, her knuckles white as she held onto the fence with her fingers. She pictured Ted's wife, lying in some small enclosure in the near future, panting, grunting, moaning. It was a woman's thing, this sound—a female thing throughout nature. She considered the helplessness of being in such a state, the black well of fear and pain there. She wondered whether Ted would hold his wife's hand during the labour. She wished Jackson would return to the helpless sow. Probably the animal was too stupid to understand why it was in so much pain. Likely, it believed it was dying—if it knew at some instinctive level what even that was.

When the sun got too hot and the farmer still hadn't returned, Claire walked to the end of the yard where an open shed stood over a rusty, mud-caked tractor and Ted's carriages—a sulky and a red buggy that had been his father's milk cart many years ago. Clambering up to the upholstered seat of the red buggy, Claire observed the pig sty, the chicken coop, and Jackson's weather-beaten house on the hill. The large, brackish pond in the middle of the barnyard had an oily green surface. Mud oozed for a few feet all around, rippling like cow-pies.

Claire stared at the mud. She felt an unbearable curiosity—an excitement that surged in her stomach, in her lower abdomen and through her thighs like illness or a sudden shock—about anything, even the mud oozing different colours. And she knew that it was a precarious, precious and fleeting gift, this way of seeing. She was different from other children; she would be different as an adult. She knew that. She looked at the adults, her father, Ted, the farmer—and wondered whether they had ever walked through the world feeling the magic that was in everything. She was not sure how to go on feeling this, ensuring that it lasted forever. It had to do with being alone; or with people, but vaguely invisible.

And if you lost this way of seeing, then being dully in a crowd would no longer matter.

The farmer was coming down from the house again, carrying the burlap sack with the leather wrapped about it. His face was redder than ever. He's been drinking while he ate lunch, Claire realized. She wanted to see the sow give birth. She had never thought too carefully about anything being born; but now, if he would let her observe. . . .

Jackson saw her on top of the milk buggy. "Get going now. Away from the barn," he waved.

Claire stepped down.

"Some things little girls shouldn't know," he said.

She stared at him. "I know more than you'd expect." She heard herself lying and left, feeling foolish. Some things I should know and Jackson shouldn't, she said to herself as she passed the farmer. She remembered her mother's story about a man where Claire's father worked. The man made his wife stand on a chair whenever she came in from shopping or from anything at all and spread her legs so he could make sure she had been faithful to him. Somehow women had no control over the things that were theirs.

The fields away from the barn were bleached yellow by the sun and too little rain. The logs in the pastures were white and smooth like the dry bones of prehistoric animals. Maybe they were bones and not logs at all. Up the hill, the barn sat like a still and silent ark. Claire watched it from one of the white logs and selected plump, green stalks of grass to pull from the ground and chew the juice out of.

These summer days were like rooms in a spacious castle. Each afternoon wrapped around her like a plump ball of baker's dough, moving, stretching out behind her. There were minutes for absorbing details— the pattern of pine trees in the woods, the way the creek sidled out narrowly from the shadows and then took on a small swallowing sound.

"Don't ever drink any of that water," Claire's mother had said one day when the family was driving up the road past the farm and they all looked at the little creek from the car window.

"Why not?" Claire wanted to know.

"I knew a girl at school once who drank water from a brook and without knowing it, she scooped up a handful of snake's eggs in the palm of her hand. Then she had those snakes growing live in her stomach."

Claire and her brother had glanced at each other in horror in the back seat, and then out the window at the retreating farm field and the creek, golden in the setting sun.

Claire pulled another stalk of grass out of the soil and began to nibble it. She imagined looking down and seeing her stomach ballooning like a watermelon and having snakes there instead of a baby.

Sitting on this log beneath the summer sky allowed one to think about who was a friend and who was not. Claire thought about her teachers. This past year, Mr. Pryde had taught a unit on horses. Knowing that Claire liked horses he had teased her in front of the class, going "Peee-yooo" and clipping his nose with a make-believe clothes peg.

She thought about her parents next, her parents' friends, her brother. She went over all the people she knew because it was too hot to enter the woods, although she often did when Jackson refused to untie Blackie. Fascinating objects appeared in the middle of nowhere— a bed spring, tires, tumbleweed-balls of barbed wire, people's clothes, empty beehives, broken balloons. And sometimes cracked cement—the remnants of a foundation where a house had stood over a hundred years ago— a place no larger than Claire's father's garage, but which had likely housed fifteen people, a mother, a father, their children being born and dying off.

There were pheasant, foxes, martens, rabbits, and, once, a deer. Claire liked to imagine riding Blackie amid the trees, sharing these various marvels with him—like the English girls photographed in *Pony Care* and *How to Train Your Horse*. She wondered about those girls with their pale serious faces, braided blond hair, and perfectly groomed ponies and stables. What were those girls doing right now? What would become of their lives?

What will become of mine? Claire wondered.

She looked at the white log she was sitting on. She thought if she looked long and hard enough at anything, she would see a mystery there. She expected to see something magical in everything. It seemed that adults went seeing without looking. Claire could not imagine walking along a street or through Jackson's barnyard or even her own home, and not peer into things. But it might come—the day might awaken when she no longer could see properly. Maybe that was what had happened to Jackson, maybe because of the woman he had once loved. That would be the worst thing—to no longer feel the electric current of exhilaration at a bone-like log lying in a field and to have no one in your life to make up for what you had lost.

Claire reached behind her and pulled at the band of her brassiere to adjust it. The boys in her class sometimes did that to a girl as a joke—snuck up and snapped her bra and then ran off hooting. The mother of one of Claire's friends had given her this bra—a hand-me-down because Claire's friend had outgrown it already.

"Show your father your new article of clothing," her mother had laughed at dinner that night, teasing.

Claire, not knowing what else to do, jerked her blouse all the way up and then down again quickly. She wished that her parents had not treated the event as an opportunity to bait her.

She walked slowly back to the barnyard, dreaming, making lists in her head. She liked to imagine winning every breed of horse that she was able to recite in one minute.

The barnyard was quiet. Ted had not arrived. Waiting for him was agonizing because there was always the possibility that her patience would not be rewarded, that he might not come at all.

There wasn't much to do with Blackie still penned up in his stall. If only she could lift her eyes and see him free in one of Jackson's distant pastures. She would call "Blackie!" and he'd come dashing—a black streak of pounding velvet mischief—and stop on a dime to rest his forehead against her upheld, unflinching palm.

She walked into the barnyard, kicking the yellow dust. Jackson was standing in the doorway of the annex. Claire stared at the heap of straw, manure, and mud lying at the edge of the oily pond. Six hairless, limp bodies were lying on top of the straw. They were piled, one piglet on top of another, curled and mute, like thawed-out chicken legs. Strange lights in the dark.

Claire looked up.

"I told you to get out of here," Jackson said, pointing his finger at her, jabbing the crooked appendage into the space in front of him. "Some things a little girl shouldn't see."

Something hard glittered in his eyes. She saw what she had always known—that he enjoyed things that were cruel. Something in him wanted the farm to fail.

"They died," Claire said, still seeing, out of the corner of her eye, the white bodies against the black.

"Not enough oxygen," Jackson shrugged. In the dark area behind him, the sow's groan sounded like a weak futile alarm. A fog horn. Claire imagined the farmer taking the baby pigs and hurling them through the air.

Kneeling on the ground, he began to scoop up their bodies from the pile. Claire looked over him into the roomy annex. Ted's horse was straining to look out over the row of empty stalls.

Claire put her hand on her stomach and pressed back a sudden twist of nausea. She believed that probably everything alive started out fair and soft and kind. She wanted Jackson to love the animals better. That was all it would take. She struggled with the words in her head, the feeling of nausea churning in her stomach as she watched the farmer's hands curl around the dead bodies. Once she had gone to his kitchen door to ask him to let Blackie loose. The farmer had put his hand on her bare arm, curled his fingers around her. She had backed away. It had been the right thing to do. He felt guilty—or afraid she'd tell her parents perhaps. He walked down to the barn with her that day and let Blackie free and the pony had raced, bucking wildly, crazily, into the south pasture where he had immediately begun to chase the cows, leaning over at a crazy angle to bite their teats.

A car pulled into the driveway by the road. Claire ran around the corner of the annex and saw Ted's station wagon, his wife beside him, and even worse, the two girls behind. Ted would have less time for talking to Claire, now. He would be distracted by his wife, his giggling daughters. He would, as he had done before when his family came with him, become slightly unrecognizable. He would ever so slightly adjust his way of talking to Claire.

Claire felt tempted to slip away before Ted spied her—into the humid, enveloping woods. She tried to decide what to do. What was there to do? She could go home and read something, or find her brother at home, unusually compatible. She looked around the barnyard searching for some kind of answer. She did not want to go home.

"You here tonight?" Ted said, coming into the yard behind her. He didn't sound annoyed or surprised. Claire thought he looked pleased. He walked ahead of his family, a long, confident, masculine stride.

"Are you taking Jewel out in the sulky or the carriage?" Claire asked shyly.

Ted rubbed his smooth chin and looked up at the sky as if the answer were there. "Sulky—how's that?" He was handsome, tanned, always even-tempered. She liked him for being sturdy, kind. He had a sideways, masculine grin like a movie star; blue eyes; a resonant, clear, man's voice.

Behind him came his wife wearing her butterfly dark glasses. Her eyebrows were pencilled a thick black. She often looked irritable as she did tonight. This was possibly Claire's fault. It was possible that Ted's wife knew exactly how Claire felt. Crossing her arms, Ted's wife rested them on the ballooning shape under her breasts and leaned against the gate. Claire smiled weakly at her. Would it be a boy or another girl? Fathers generally seemed prouder to have sons. Henry VIII cut off the heads of wives that didn't have boys.

Jackson had cleared the baby pigs away. Claire looked at the heap of discoloured hay—faint impressions where the bodies had lain. She followed Ted into the annex. When he had first moved Jewel into Jackson's barn, Claire had hoped conditions might change for the better. She had thought that Ted might speak up on her and Blackie's behalf and see that Blackie was cared for properly, exercised, fed molasses mixed with oats for his coat the way Jewel was.

"The sow had her litter today," she told Ted. "They all died."

He wasn't listening. Jewel twisted on her rope to watch him. "Move over," Ted said, pushing her flank. He took the jar filled with molasses and began to rub some into her shining bronze-coloured coat.

The sow had her babies in this stall next to Jewel," Claire pointed. "Jackson threw the bodies out this door. I saw them."

"Did he?" Ted shot a look at her. "Wonder why he'd do a thing like that?"

Claire tried to think how to put it better—the thing she had really seen. Words were confounding. It was impossible to say what she wanted, what she saw, what she feared. Words jumped like Mexican beans in her head. She was unsure how to take control of them.

"Nice evening, isn't it?" Ted said.

"Yes." Claire looked at her hands. She leapt aside as Jewel swung about being backed out of her stall. Her hoofs lifted and settled restlessly.

Outside, as Ted pulled the sulky out of the shed, his wife came over to stroke Jewel's nose. "Why are her eyes rolling like that, Ted?" she asked. She drew back and folded her arms over her sweater again. She smiled at Claire. "How's your mother these days?"

"She's fine," Claire replied, avoiding her eyes. Her mother was the same age as these people. Perhaps her mother could have married Ted if fate had been different. Claire glanced sharply at Ted's profile. She was glad he wasn't her father. She stared at his wife's stomach and felt a keen, sharp pain in her chest at the thought of her mother having another child. She knew, of course, how it happened—but the thought of this union between her mother and father was unpleasant, a feeling of strain in the house. When their dog was still alive, he had wrapped his paws around people's legs and rubbed himself. Claire and her brother had screamed with laughter for years, calling it "the kangaroo" game.

Jewel moved her hind legs in arcs about the ground while her harness was fastened to the sulky—a labyrinth of straps, lengths of leather, buckles. Ted drew a strap from her forehead to her back to keep her head from bobbing. "She's all right," he said. "It's been three nights since she was out—cooped up in the barn all day."

"How do you think Blackie feels?" Claire blurted out. As Ted looked sheepish, she felt her face redden. She didn't want to make him feel guilty. But she herself felt ashamed at being in the yard amid the finery of the sulky with Jewel groomed and looking like a show horse. She imagined breaking the pony's rope, letting him race in a frenzy all over the place, out to the edges of Jackson's property.

I should do it now, she thought, with Ted here so that Jackson can't do anything about it.

"I don't understand why the hell Jackson keeps that horse."

"Ted!" his wife said.

They glanced at each other. They were never very comfortable. Ted was a different person when his wife accompanied him. Neither of them smiled at each other. They did not hold hands or laugh together in the secret way that married people did in the movies. People's marriages were generally an effort. Claire felt secretly pleased at the look on Ted's wife's face.

Skirting the brackish pond, she wandered down to the furthest door of the barn to look into the gloom at Blackie. He twisted on his rope to regard her. She looked up at the cobwebs and across the empty stalls to the mad bull. She thought about prisons she had seen before—the one in Guelph, Alcatraz in a picture, the story of the Tower of London in the Grade four textbook. Prisons were often set in dazzling surroundings—on hills overlooking forests and rivers, on islands overlooking a city such as San Francisco. Claire knew that if she were ever a horse and tied to a stall for weeks on end, or a prisoner in the Tower of London like Mary, Queen of Scots, she would definitely lose her mind. It would be better to be imprisoned in a room with no window.

She wandered back to the yard where Jewel had been backed into the two arms of the sulky.

"Want to take the reins tonight?" Ted asked.

Claire's anger subsided. "OK." She helped him buckle up. Occasionally, he glanced at her and smiled, or

71

asked her to name a part of the harness. Jewel's hoofs danced as if the ground were fiery, her ears swept back.

"I'll take her around once alone," Ted said when the sulky was prepared.

"No, let me ride with you," Claire said. She had to put a hand up for him to help her, and the feel of his skin made her dizzy with nervousness. She had never seen anyone with eyes as blue as Ted's. It was a man like this that she wanted to marry some day.

She didn't say anything as they drove out. Ted struggled to hold the horse to a walk.

The sun was slipping beneath the horizon. Too fast to ever catch it. A gold light veiled the pine trees and the creek. Claire pictured that same light falling on a nestle of tiny snake eggs, round and gleaming as pearls.

"We're entering Jewel in the Orono Fair in September," Ted said once they were going at an even pace. The sulky's wheels creaked over the soft, crackling ground.

"Are you?" Claire said. What did "we" mean?

"Ask your Mum and Dad if you can come along."

"Oh I can," Claire said firmly. She jumped ahead to imagine the day, the taffy apples and hot dog booths, rows of horses and saddles, the owners and spectators milling about, the familiar sweet-and-sour envy that she always experienced around people with horses. But she would be with Ted and his horse, and maybe his wife and two girls would decide not to come.

"We'll be renting a trailer and loading Jewel that morning," Ted continued. "But not from here. I'm not happy with the way Jackson cleans out the stalls here. He leaves a lot to be desired. We've got a new stall lined up."

He leaves a lot. . . . Claire's heart lurched crazily in her chest. "Where?"

He named a farm much further north.

"Anyway, Jackson's giving this place up, you know. The City wants its land back. They're building a highschool for you kids."

She was thankful that Ted knew not to look at her. The idea of highschool terrified her—the lockers, the brusque older students, tougher standards, dances. The feeling she had been experiencing all day, that she couldn't get enough of the farm, rose in her throat. She studied Ted's strong forearms, tensing and rippling beside her as he struggled with the reins. She looked at his fingernails. They were perfect and gleaming, with white moons. He smelled of coffee and shaving cream. She would work something out, arrange to get out to the new farm—maybe arrange to get Blackie out there as well. A pointless dream.

She looked behind her to watch the lip of the sun resting on the edge of the earth. She hoped that in heaven she might meet up again with the animals she had loved—the way they were before they had become ill or ruined, Blackie, pet cats and dogs, the deer that her father had struck one night with his car and left at the side of the road.

The farm was to be sold; on this very ground she would be walking along corridors and studying physics, chemistry, biology—remote worlds of harsh metal and gaseous odours. She would still be Ted's friend. She glanced up at his face.

He guided Jewel in a wide circle at the foot of the field and headed back for the barnyard. His two little girls were giggling by the gate ahead. The youngest one was waving a scarf. Once, Claire had run into Jackson's field waving her scarf, and the cows that Jackson was trying to herd into a pen disbanded in all directions. He had been furious with her that day. She had let a week go by before returning.

"Someone else's turn," Ted said as they approached the barn yard. "You'll get another turn at it, don't worry," he winked at Claire.

She looked ahead and saw Ted's daughter and

the scarf.

"Don't, that'll frighten Jewel," Claire shouted.

Abruptly, she was thrown back as Jewel leapt ahead. For a second, the horse was frozen in mid-air, in an unnatural capriole. Then she began to gallop, a frenzied, panic-stricken break to escape, her haunches lowered. In surging, neck-wrenching bolts, she galloped wildly into the barn yard, flashing past Ted's gasping wife, her arms wrapped tightly around the two girls. The sulky swerved crazily.

"Get out! Jump!" Ted yelled.

Claire looked at the ground, blurred and distant. She hung tightly to the sulky, her eyes riveted to the surging back of the horse, moving now at a fast gallop about the small barnyard, like an animal struggling to get out of deep water. Claire felt a shriek of laughter bursting in her throat—Jewel looked so desperate, so foolish and trapped.

She hung onto the sides of the sulky until suddenly a carriage wheel caught a board on the lean-to shed. A tearing noise ripped through the air and the sulky jarred to one side, throwing Claire off her seat. For one horrifying moment, she thought she would land in the pond. A sickening, heavy sensation swept through her body as she hit the oily green mud at the edge.

Suddenly, Jackson was there. He had a crusty, stained towel which he was using to rub mud from Claire's shirt in rough polishing motions. Through her shock, Claire could see Ted up on his heels, leaning backwards like a charioteer, pulling with all his weight. Through a watery screen, she heard him calling "Whoa!"

"I'm all right," Claire said to Jackson, shuddering at the dull pain beneath her skin. She hated the farmer to be so close, his earth-stained hands touching her. He lifted Claire's tee shirt to her chin and stared at her. She pushed her shirt down again. "Don't," she said, trembling, drawing away from him. Jackson grinned. She

74

had never seen that before—a grin like this, wide, toothless, with raw, sore-looking gums like a horse's mouth.

Ted had managed to rein Jewel in and was unharnessing her. Claire stood up. She walked through a grey watery haze past Ted's wife, who was saying something. Forcing herself to go on walking, she followed Ted into the annex as he led Jewel to her stall. The horse was flecked with foam. Claire leaned against the wall and slid down till she was resting on the straw-covered floor. She thought perhaps a rib was broken, or her stomach crushed. She wondered what would happen if she simply, stubbornly, remained at the farm until she died.

"You all right?" Ted said, frowning.

Claire nodded. She felt frightened by his grim, tight-lipped silence—and taken aback that he was no more concerned about her than that. She felt a funny sensation around her heart—a squeezing dark pain that made her want to cry out, to beg for something. It flashed through her mind that she was responsible for this disaster—she had shouted to Ted's daughter and that might have frightened Jewel, more than the waving handkerchief.

"We'll be waiting in the car, Ted," his wife said from the opening to the annex. "You all right?" she said to Claire. Her pencilled black eyebrows lifted like wings. She had learned it before; but each time, the truth struck Claire with a terrible, wounding force—how little people felt or cared, how on her own she was. She stared at Ted's wife and nodded. The woman pressed her lips into a funny smile. Claire stared at her lips, wrinkled and purple, the thin skin looking bruised, like an over-ripe prune.

It was getting dark. The inside of the barn was chilly. The straw and wood had turned dull grey with sunset. She didn't want to stay and see what Ted was going to do, but she was afraid to leave the farm with things unsettled, unwitnessed. She felt reckless and torn inside.

Ted tied Jewel to the head of her stall. He removed a thick, two-foot length of rubber hanging from a nail and raised his arm in the air. The strap came down against the horse's haunches. Jewel thudded against the side of her stall, shocked. "Whoa!" Ted cried. He brought the rubber strap down again. "Whoa!"

Claire watched and waited, stunned, disbelieving. It stunned her to see his face look righteous as he beat his horse. She felt herself losing interest in Jewel. The animal was ruined for her now. Claire watched herself, bewildered at the swift extinguishing of her interest in Jewel.

It was dark when Ted left. Claire watched him pack things up. He was like an adult again, a stranger.

"See you next week," he said, not looking at her. His hands folded into fists and opened again.

Claire had never been at the farm this late before. She wondered why Ted, who lived two blocks away, didn't offer to give her a ride home. She would have said, No thank you. She didn't want to be in the car with his daughters who would still be giggling despite the terrible thing that had befallen their father's horse. Her mother would be angry that she was home so late, that she had not asked Ted for a lift home.

In the lean-to shed, Claire sat on the red carriage. One of Jackson's windows was lit. When she had gone to his kitchen door that time, she had seen that the linoleum was black with soot, no furniture, nothing but a table and a chair with a piece of oilcloth on it. She had seen Jackson's nephew once—a tall, too-thin, pimply boy a few years older than Claire. She had even seen the saddle Jackson had bought his nephew—a foolish, ornate Western saddle with an enormous horn and fake rhinestones down the stirrup. The farm was going to be sold. Soon someone else would take over Blackie's care. She wondered idly if the pony would pass his life tied up in crumbling barns.

She wandered out to the road and looked down its length of dusty grass and, in the distance, the trimmed green of people's lawns. She decided to return through the woods. She had already missed dinner and for this she would be punished. Her mother would likely disappear into a cold silence that might last for weeks, and her father—she would have disappointed and angered him yet again. She dragged her feet through the fading grass and studied the contour of the land as she approached the woods. She knew each bump in the soil, each falling fence post, each clump of dandelion and devil's paintbrush. Ahead of her, the woods looked too dark to walk through. Sounds would echo differently. She felt hungry for the dinner she had missed, and thirsty. The creek idled duskily along its banks. Stooping, Claire ladled some water into her palm. She studied it intently and then, leaning over, sipped it.

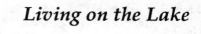
Living on the Lake

On the first day of spring, Lilah waited in the school playground for Suzette. They were in different grades, since Lilah was two years younger. Suzette's Grade 8 class was serving a ten-minute detention for throwing spit balls.

A number of bikes were lined up beside the school, their plastic streamers were snapping in the breeze. Lilah could hear the city, its electric, smoky roar, several miles to the west. Thinking about the people who lived in the city made her feel impatient. Even this— seeing the coloured strips of plastic flap in the air and waiting for Suzette—filled her with an unbearable restlessness.

Suzette finally emerged from the school and they began to walk home.

"Look who's waiting for us," Lilah said, once they had left the school grounds and were walking along the sidewalk.

Suzette peered along the sidewalk. Her eyes narrowed and she nudged Lilah. "Do you want to?"

Further along, Mr. Sherman was trimming the cedar bush that bordered the sidewalk. He scissored the air with the garden shears as he spied the two girls coming toward him. His pale whiskered face brightened and he waved.

Looking beyond him, Lilah could see the lake on

the horizon, as still as the backdrop in an old movie, an unwrinkled robin's egg blue. She began to imagine situations—adventures where she might be forced to row across it as a matter of life or death.

Suzette cut into her thoughts. "Don't start laughing."

"I won't. Don't forget—you only see him at his house. I have to be an actress on Sundays."

Lilah went to church with her mother. Every Sunday, they entered the yellow foyer, and Mr. Sherman, in his suit and tie and VO5-slicked hair, escorted her mother to a pew near the front. It was difficult for Lilah not to glance at him and start to smirk. She enjoyed the possibility of being caught sending such a look in Sherman's direction.

Three pews ahead, Mrs. Sherman always sat waiting for her husband to finish his tasks in the church foyer and join her for the service. She was a fat, dwarf-like woman with bow legs and a churchwoman's bosom that rested on her protruding stomach. Every Sunday, she pivoted in her seat and looked through her watery, vague glasses to see who was at church. Then she'd see Lilah and Mrs. Arliss and give them a wan smile.

It was hard to say how much she knew.

Suzette's parents never went to church. They fought a lot. Even worse, Mrs. Braun had to work, a situation considered suspect by the other neighbourhood women.

"Do you ever see Suzette's father?" Mrs. Arliss had asked Lilah once.

"Sometimes."

"Don't ever go into his and Mrs. Braun's bedroom or lie down on their bed. Not for any reason," Mrs. Arliss said.

"Why?"

Mrs. Arliss had pursed her lips and looked at the wall beside the kitchen table. "There's a gun under his pillow. He keeps it because of something that happened years ago."

Lilah struggled not to appear over-anxious.

"What?"

"He was in love with some girl and her family wouldn't let them marry. So they agreed to die together and Matt Braun drove his car over a cliff down at the lake. Only the girl died and he didn't. Her brothers swore they'd kill Matt Braun for it. So he sleeps with a gun under his pillow."

Lilah wished she had the nerve to slip into the Braun's bedroom some time and look under both pillows—or the nerve to ask Suzette if the story was true. But what if it wasn't? The Brauns lived in a way that was unpredictable, but carefree, energetic. Lilah liked to visit such disorderliness. Someone was always coming or going; there was always trouble or laughter.

"Come in for a glass of milk," Mr. Sherman said when Lilah and Suzette were closer on the sidewalk. "Or for a cup of tea," he added.

A sly trick. Lilah was not allowed to drink tea at home and he knew it. Suzette could do anything she liked because her mother worked. She was the middle of five sisters—all blonde, blue-eyed girls—and she wasn't scrutinized the way Lilah was, an only child whose mother stayed at home.

The girls unhooked arms. Suzette spoke in the aggressive voice she had recently started to cultivate. "We'll take tea. We can't stay long. Is Mrs. Sherman at home?"

Lilah glanced at her, flushing. Suzette was direct about what she wanted.

Mr. Sherman winked. "Shopping. You can say hello when she gets back."

He led them up the side stairs to the kitchen door. They followed him inside and Lilah started to tremble with a pleasurable mix of reluctance and excitement.

As usual, an odour permeated the house, as if a wet dog had run through it. But the Shermans no longer kept pets—not since their two daughters had gone off with men to have their own children. Evidently, they had owned a parakeet once, but now the cage sat beside Mrs. Sherman's purple velvet armchair with a Boston fern growing out of it. The house was stuffy. Nothing looked overly clean. At home, Lilah could see her reflection in the yellow paint of her mother's kitchen cupboards.

At the kitchen table, Mr. Sherman sat down on a chair and Suzette and Lilah got up on his lap, one on each broad knee. Suzette turned the pages of the magazine so that he could keep one hand beneath each of them, balancing them. The pictures in the magazine depicted women with black bands painted over the photograph to conceal their eyes. They had enormous breasts and thin strips of white fabric stretched tautly between their legs.

After a few minutes, Lilah could feel Mr. Sherman's fingers pressing up between her legs. No one said anything. It irritated her that he thought she and Suzette didn't realize what he was doing, but other times, she wished he would be dirtier, more dangerous—actually touch her skin instead of push through her underwear. She wondered what would take place if Mrs. Sherman walked in and saw the look on her husband's face.

After they had looked at the pictures of women tied with ropes, or leaning toward the camera with their breasts hugged together, he fixed them a cup of tea.

"You won't tell Mrs. Sherman, will you?" he said, as they left by the side door. He was confident of their loyalty—or of their stupidity. Lilah couldn't be sure which.

She and Suzette walked to the playhouse in Lilah's back yard. Originally, it had been a shed for Mr. Arliss's lawnmower. Now, it consisted of a table and two chairs, a square piece of linoleum, and a small rug. Their supplies included a flashlight, which Lilah had found as the prize in a box of popcorn, a package of dates and bottles of Orange Crush. They had made curtains and put up pictures of Joanne Woodward and Angie Dickenson wearing black-net nylons and lacy bathing suits. The door had a lock on it.

They kept their mothers' cast-off dresses here, as well: taffeta evening dresses, and a glamorous blue satin gown that Suzette's mother had given them—all with crinolines and fancy cloth-covered buttons. Lilah often pictured Suzette's mother in that fairytale blue dress. Maybe she had been wearing it the night Mr. Braun fell in love with her.

Some days, if they got bored, they put these dresses on and took pictures of each other. On Lilah, the dresses looked like housecoats. The strapless ones slipped to her waist. On Suzette, who was fifty pounds heavier, a few dresses were tight and she had trouble getting the zippers done up. Sometimes, she split an entire seam. But in most of the dresses, she looked like a woman.

"Let's go to Toronto on the train," Suzette said as Lilah counted the money they had saved and tapped it into a neat bundle on the playhouse floor. "We can take the subway to Yorkville and get into a bar."

Lilah leaned against the playhouse wall and thought about that. The truth was, she didn't care about getting into bars. She liked to think about taking a bus to Niagara Falls and listening to the thunder, and walking through the Chamber of Horrors at the wax museum where there was a display of Charles Blondin riding his bicycle over the treacherous gorge.

"You know what I'd really like to do—save this and wait until Nancy Sinatra's new movie comes."

"I'll take my half and go to Yorkville alone," Suzette grumbled.

* * *

When the weekend came, Lilah walked over to Suzette's. Along the way, she thought about Mrs. Braun who was always laughing and who, for years, had made the best Freshie and the best popcorn in the neighbourhood for whoever happened to drop in to see one of her daughters. She was always tanned and happy.

"Don't get married!" she always laughed. "Just go out with boys."

"What about having children?" Lilah asked her once.

"Don't ever have children."

The Brauns lived on the shore of Lake Ontario in a large white house with green shutters. One of the stairways inside was blocked off by boards. Lilah often wondered why this had been done—and who had nailed the boards up like that? Boxes sat everywhere, unpacked since the Brauns had moved in five years earlier. The walls in many rooms were half-wallpapered, with bright modern paper ending where the old pattern remained, faded and water-stained.

As Lilah walked up the driveway, she looked at the mist-enveloped lake in front of the house and thought about Rochester and the rest of New York State, mysterious and foreign on the opposite side. Water meant all sorts of things: marauding pirates, yachts and millionaires, journeys, drowning, mermaids, monsters, submarines that were silent and lethal. Oysters with pearls inside.

Two years before, on April 1, the local paper had published a picture of a monster like Godzilla rising out of the lake. On page 2, they had printed, "Happy April Fool's Day." Lilah had felt disappointed. She liked to think that if she watched the lake closely and often enough, a real monster, like the one in Loch Ness, might reveal itself. She was glad that someone she knew lived on the water.

Angela, the youngest Braun, was lying on the

hammock in the long, green yard. Her caramel-coloured hair tumbled over the side of the canvas. She saw Lilah, yawned, and didn't speak. Another sister, Annie, was in the kitchen cooking french fries in a pot that was smoking and hissing. The house smelled like a chip truck.

"Come on up, Lilah," Suzette called from upstairs.

In the living room, a sofa and three chairs were covered with white sheets. In front of the fireplace, a large picture leaned against the bricks. Lilah stopped to look at it each time she visited—a photograph taken years ago of the five Braun girls, each sister like a blond, blue-eyed princess in a fairy tale with their creamy faces and pale pink smocked dresses, ribbons and lace at their necks and wrists.

On the way upstairs, Lilah passed the oldest sister, Maria, who was sixteen. She was going on dates now and wore lipstick that smelled like pink candy floss. In her drawers, there were lacy push-up bras with rose sachets inside the cups. Her current boyfriend was much older; he aspired to be like Bob Dylan. He had long curly hair, smoked, didn't say anything, scowled, played a guitar.

Maria looked at Lilah warily and said "hello" as if it were beneath her, but the cultured thing to do.

"What took you so long?" Suzette said at her bedroom door. Once Lilah was inside, she pushed the knob in to lock the door.

"I had to wash the cellar stairs. It's one of my new chores."

Suzette made a face and shrugged. "Come on," she said, bouncing on her double bed as she kicked off her slippers.

Lilah lay down on the bed and took her clothes off. She watched Suzette undress. Under the bedspread, they started to wrestle, laughing when one got too rough. Sometimes, they stopped to kiss each other's neck. Lilah breathed in the honey and rose scent of Suzette's new round breasts. She arched her back and moaned, pressing her head into the pillow as Suzette explored with her fingers.

"Do you want to use something?" Suzette asked.

Over the past few years, they had used a feather, a carrot, and a ruler.

A rap at the door startled them. Lilah stared at Suzette.

"What are you two doing in there?" Maria demanded from the hall.

"We're doing what's none of your god-damned business," Suzette said loudly, narrow-eyed.

"Open this door!" Maria rattled the knob.

"Eat shit!"

Maria pounded on the door and Lilah sat up, quickly pulling her jeans on. Suzette lay back on the bed, laughing. She stared tauntingly at the door and laughed like crazy.

They listened as Maria stomped downstairs.

Suzette looked at Lilah. "Don't get dressed. Let's go for a swim. I'll lend you a suit."

Lilah considered. "What if your mother hears that we've been in the lake?"

"She won't. She's not home for two hours yet."

"Maria will tell her," Lilah pointed out, but she had already taken her blouse off again.

"She wouldn't dare. I'll tell Mum that she sleeps around and that she keeps safes in her purse."

The water was cold. Lilah went in up to her knees and stopped. She was terrified of getting caught by the strong undertow that tugged at her ankles like a stranger's hands. She stood in anxious amazement and watched Suzette, who kept disappearing behind the waves and bobbing up again.

* * *

When she got home, Lilah's mother was making a stew at the stove. "I don't like your going to the Brauns when neither of those parents are ever at home," she said as soon as Lilah had hung her jacket up.

Lilah's heart began to beat faster. Another freedom was about to be taken away—another escape was about to be sealed off and she would be pushed further into the strenuous place of lying convincingly, into taking even greater risks.

"Mrs. Braun always calls to see if anyone needs anything," she lied.

Mrs. Arliss looked up from the steaming pot. "Did she today?"

"She phoned before I arrived—Annie said so." She always left herself a way out.

"If I ever hear that you go near the lake, I'll forbid you to even see Suzette. I don't understand why the Brauns bought that place, what they could have been thinking of. Typical of those two, though."

"We don't go near the lake."

"Well, don't. What do you do over there?" Mrs. Arliss asked more congenially.

"The same sort of thing we do in the playhouse."

All evening, Lilah worried that Suzette's mother would call. She lay awake worrying and planning after she had gone to bed. She was not much of a sleeper anyway, because she imagined too much. The direction her life was taking and the remote world of being an adult were the two things that kept her awake wondering.

Long after midnight, she was often still awake, listening to her transistor radio. One night, under her blanket, she had heard Skeeter Davis sing, "The End of the World." Lilah kept hearing the song in her memory. She hoped she would never be as hopeless and lonely as Skeeter Davis sounded.

Tonight, lying awake listening to her transistor,

Lilah heard Nancy Sinatra singing, "These Boots Are Made For Walking." Sitting up in bed, Lilah listened to it. She wished she could be in the song, or the one singing it. She envisioned herself dressed like Nancy—in white go-go boots and a tight white and black mini dress. After the song had ended, Lilah sat up in her dark bedroom, holding on to the sense of power the music gave her.

The next morning at breakfast, keeping her voice even, Lilah announced to her mother that she planned to buy the record.

"I don't like the Sinatras—they're tied up with organized crime. It's a fact," Mrs. Arliss said. "Anyway, I don't want you buying records—there's plenty of time for that. Save your money."

"It's my money," Lilah said, feeling herself heading toward a red, dangerous anger.

She sold Regal Christmas cards and every January ended up with a box of one and two dollar bills. She had an allowance too and occasionally she took extra change from her mother's purse when sent to the store. Having money set aside gave her a greater sense of safety.

"Save it—you can buy me a nice Christmas present," Mrs. Arliss joked.

"The same thing happened when I wanted to buy 'Blame It On the Bossa Nova'."

"That's an adult song and you're not going to buy adult records," Mrs. Arliss said, flying into her own red fury.

They eyed each other warily. Any moment something uncomfortable and awful might be said. Lilah would say "I hate you" in a strangled voice. Her mother would threaten to ship Lilah off to a private girls school where no privileges were granted at all. The same argument had taken place over a Christmas record, "Winter Wonderland," because the singer and his girl were "conspiring" by the fire. That time, Lilah bought the record anyway, but it was a pointless purchase because she couldn't very well play it. The record was buried in thick plastic in the backyard behind the playhouse. Many things were buried there.

Once, when she was upset over something, Lilah had collected the jewellery she had received at Christmas and birthdays, plus a few things from her mother's dresser. She put the necklaces, bracelets, and earrings into a plastic bag and left it on the back porch while she went down to her father's work room for a shovel. She liked the idea of buried treasure. It was a secret over which she would have complete control. She began to plan a cryptic map that people would discover hundreds of years in the future. When she came upstairs, the bag was gone from the back porch.

Two years ago, she came across one of the bracelets lying in the spring mud at the foot of a tree in the backyard. She wondered sometimes whether she had buried the treasure that day after all and just forgot. It surprised her that her mother never noticed the missing items.

* * *

Lilah and Suzette were sitting in the playhouse. It was August now. Through the window, the sky looked humid and grey. They were putting in the hours. The movie with Nancy Sinatra was playing downtown.

"These Boots Are Made For Walking" came on the transistor radio and Lilah turned it up.

"Do you like it?" she asked Suzette.

"It's all right," Suzette said. "I like 'Sally, Go Round the Roses' better."

"As though Sally would go through the roses," Lilah said darkly.

Suzette laughed. She wanted to go back to talking about how to kiss someone. "After you kiss a guy, you're supposed to keep your eyes closed for ten seconds to look romantic."

"And to get your bearings," Lilah added.

"Well, I don't know," Suzette said doubtfully. She studied her fingernails.

Earlier that morning, they had gone to Mr. Sherman's. His wife was at home, sitting in her chair sewing buttons. Telling her that he was going out to show the girls his vegetable garden, he took Lilah and Suzette to the hot, dusty loft over his garage. The three of them sat in the yellow straw and he gave them a calendar with a photo of a woman wearing a cowboy hat and a low-cut top, a Macaw perched on her arm.

"It's for the playhouse I keep hearing about," he told them.

"What a colourful bird," Suzette said coyly, darting a look at Lilah.

Mr. Sherman laughed at her. "You like more than the bird."

Under the straw, in one corner of the loft, he had hidden a stack of magazines. He got one out and sat on the straw-covered floor. Lilah and Suzette arranged themselves on his lap and Lilah turned the pages, her fingers trembling as Mr. Sherman's fingers curled under the tight crotch of her underwear and began to stroke the damp skin. A deep, urgent feeling came over her. She felt her underpants grow warm and wet. She flashed a look at him. He looked back at her in a pleased, knowing way. She realized, glancing then at Suzette's face, that this was how Suzette had been responding all along. At that moment, Suzette dropped the magazine and slapped her hand tightly over his, pressing against herself. Lilah sat consumed with heat and a moan trapped in her throat as the old man pushed his finger all the way up. When they left the garage, she avoided his eyes and watched Suzette instead, who punched Mr. Sherman's arm in a light, familiar way and chattered on about seeing him again.

Lilah lay on her back on the playhouse floor and

91

looked up at the calendar, thumbtacked alongside a picture of Marilyn Monroe, who had recently killed herself. She thought about Mr. Sherman and how much she disliked him for laughing at Suzette, for thinking that they were too innocent, too stupid, to know what was going on. His marriage and his life could be ruined by just one breath of the truth to Mrs. Arliss. He'd no longer be standing in the church foyer on Sunday mornings.

Suzette took a bottle of nail polish from the shelf. She began to apply the enamel to her nails. For two weeks, they had been talking about how they might possibly get into the restricted Nancy Sinatra movie.

Several days before, they had taken a bus downtown. In Woolworths, they bought pink nailpolish, two pairs of fishnet nylons, two kerchiefs that looked like bits of cirrus cloud, and garter belts for the nylons. From their mothers' bathrooms, they borrowed circles of rouge and pressed powder. And they each had a blue, Empire-waistline dress to wear.

* * *

After dinner, they walked downtown, carrying the make-up, hairspray and their outfits in plastic bags. It was light out till late now. At the dinner table, Lilah had told her parents she was playing baseball at the park—a risky story, because sometimes her father got it into his head to walk down and watch her.

"Do you really think this is going to work?" Lilah asked Suzette on their way downtown.

"It will."

"No matter how much make-up we put on, anyone will see how young we are up close."

Suzette laughed and slapped her plastic bag against her leg. "Men like young girls," she said. She looked away—at nothing, but at something she had seen or heard before.

Lilah was silent for several blocks. Suzette was not afraid of men. For Lilah, they were vaguely threatening, unpredictable.

"A man can't stop himself if you let him get past a certain point," Mrs. Arliss often pointed out. And she told Lilah, "A woman never enjoys sex as much as a man."

Men had no control over their bodies or their minds, Mrs. Arliss said. But Mr. Sherman wasn't letting things go too far—although he probably imagined it. And Lilah was sure that Mrs. Braun enjoyed sex. There was that cheerfulness and pink, plump prettiness about her that made Lilah feel this had to be the truth. And she had given birth to the five daughters.

At one of the hotels along the main street, Suzette and Lilah changed their clothes in the women's washroom. A dispenser produced a vial of Paris cologne for twenty-five cents. They dabbed some on and made their faces up, hiding in the cubicles each time the door opened and a woman came in. When they were finished, they checked themselves in the mirror over the sinks, standing on toilet seats with the doors held back to see as much as possible of their legs. With the face powder and tight dresses, they looked older.

"I bet we could even get into a bar," Suzette said confidently.

Lilah rolled her eyes. That would be pushing things too far.

They had taken two pairs of Maria's high-heeled shoes, and as they emerged from the hotel, Lilah felt herself teetering ridiculously. Her feet were long and narrow, and Maria's shoes were for plump short feet like Suzette's. Like Mrs. Braun's. And anyway, Lilah had never worn heels before.

"Now what?" Lilah asked nervously.

"Let's just wait here like I said," Suzette said. She leaned against the hotel wall with her arms folded.

"Guys go driving around—someone will stop and ask what we're doing." She wasn't nervous, but her voice sounded edgy and sarcastic.

"We have to be careful." Lilah leaned against the wall with her arms behind her. The brick felt warm and smooth.

"You're always so frightened." The make-up made Suzette's nose and chin, even her eyelids, look sharp and pale. A film of powder dusted her lashes.

"I am not," Lilah said. She resolved not to be visibly afraid and ruin their chances of being escorted into the restricted movie.

"What can happen?" Suzette went on. "We're going to meet a couple of guys, go to your stupid movie—then go home."

"Imagine if Sherman saw us here," Lilah said. "He'd figure it's all right to finger us."

"He already thinks it's OK," Suzette observed.

Lilah flashed a look sideways. "He does not."

They were quiet for a moment. Lilah felt bewildered by the sudden strain. "Imagine doing this for real," she said.

Suzette sounded really irritated. "We are doing it for real."

Lilah struggled. "I mean being sixteen."

She felt as if she were losing some sort of control. She didn't feel liked suddenly, not on even footing. She remembered her mother's warning that Suzette would go to highschool in the fall and, that after that, they wouldn't really be friends.

"Look at Maria—who wants to be sixteen?" Suzette said, glowering down the street toward a line of cars that had started up as the lights turned green. "I told her and her boyfriend last night that it's a miracle she isn't pregnant yet."

"You said that in front of him?" Lilah demanded. There was something vivid and truthful about the open

94

anger between the Brauns that she liked.

Suzette smiled and took a tube of lipstick from her purse. She regarded her reflection in a compact mirror, the lipstick poised over her lips. "They both wanted to kill me. It's probably already true."

She snapped the compact shut. Lilah pulled her eyes from Suzette's face and followed her gaze to a car pulling up at the curb. In it were two men with short-sleeve shirts, short hair. The man driving leaned out the window. "Want to go for a ride?"

"Can't. We're taking in a movie. Want to come?" Suzette smiled.

The two men spoke to each other and one of the laughed. Lilah felt her stomach flip-flop.

"Hold on," the driver said, winking at them.

They parked their car at the gas station across the street. When they got out, Suzette began to sputter. "Look at them!"

The men were wearing plaid Bermuda shorts, athletic ankle socks, and sneakers. When they jogged across the intersection, they looked like conservative older men. Like teachers.

"When they get up close, they'll see how young we are," Lilah whispered.

"Just keep your mouth shut and they'll never know," Suzette instructed. "They'll get us into your movie—that's what you want, isn't it?"

At the ticket booth, Lilah hung back and tried to make her face wear an older girl's expression. She remembered coming here with Suzette a year ago to see Walt Disney's "The Nine Lives of Thomasina." While everyone else in the theatre had cried at the cat's funeral, Suzette had laughed so hard she was practically screaming.

The tickets were purchased through the wicket, no questions asked. In the foyer, Bob, who had been driving and who was clearly going to be Suzette's boyfriend tonight, drew out a pack of cigarettes. Everyone took one. When Lilah inhaled for the first time, she felt her body wanting to slump to the floor to go to sleep.

The posters for "The Wild Angels" showed Peter Fonda and Nancy Sinatra on motorcycles, with Nancy in her mini-skirt and high-heeled boots. The ads reminded Lilah of the local motorcycle gang—a dirty, dangerous-looking mob of men who were half-ridiculous, half-terrifying. There were even some older men who had never gotten free of being like boys or thugs, who still wore the jackets, rode the bikes, and lived in falling-down cottages on the outskirts of town.

Lilah felt tired suddenly. She knew that if things got very bad, desperate, she could always call her father and face the music. She realized that Suzette was much more on her own—she both had to and could afford to be as reckless as she pleased. Lilah pictured her father walking to the park at this moment and seeing there was no baseball practice. Suppose he decided to drive through town looking for her.

Suzette was holding hands with Bob, the driver. The second man, Glenn, was sullen. He studied the posters of Nancy and Peter, and looked at Lilah as if she were an idiot when she asked him, "Have you heard her sing?" He and Lilah avoided looking at each other after that, even when he had to hand her a bottle of orange crush and a box of popcorn that Bob had bought. She realized he knew he'd been tricked. She felt ashamed for him. They walked down the aisle of the theatre in silence behind Suzette, who now had her arm through Bob's. Lilah felt like reaching forward and pinching her.

The movie began and Lilah tried to concentrate. She wondered what it was that she had expected from the movie. The black leather boots made Nancy look tough and sexy, but she didn't seem able to stand up straight in them. She and Peter Fonda danced and smoked mari-juana at a funeral with their dead motorcycle friend propped against a wall, a lit cigarette in his mouth. Even after he had hit her, Nancy went on loving Peter Fonda.

Lilah shifted uneasily in her seat. The garter belt was biting into her flesh and the high heels were cutting off the circulation in her feet. She wondered how well she was going to adapt to fashion. She fought the impulse to nudge Suzette and ask questions about the movie's plot, which was muddled and perplexing.

Suzette had missed most of the show. She was turned in her seat, kissing Bob. Lilah could tell by the pauses that Suzette was keeping her eyes closed for ten seconds after each kiss. Glenn leaned toward the aisle with his chin in his hand. Once, he let out a furious sigh. Lilah's face darkened in confusion. There was nothing she could say to him. It occurred to her that the movie would be soon over, and she would be manoeuvred by Suzette's looks into the back seat of Bob's car with the surly Glenn.

Her eyes fell on a couple several rows ahead. From behind, with her curling blond hair and pink, fleshy arm stretched along the back of the seat and cradling the man's shoulder, the woman looked like Suzette. Lilah blinked and stared as the woman moved her head slightly. It was Maria and her boyfriend, who looked like Bob Dylan. Maria shifted in her seat slightly to make some space and her boyfriend slipped his hand into her blouse. He glanced at the rows of seats behind him—not secretively or suspiciously, but as if to confirm that he and Maria were being observed. That was what he cared about.

Panic rustled through Lilah's body. She stood up and slid past Glenn's knees without a word. Looking back, she saw that Suzette hadn't noticed she was leaving. Or maybe she had but it wasn't important compared to necking with Bob.

In the theatre's washroom, Lilah splashed water on her face and removed the nylons and garter belt.

Immediately, she felt safer. She put her runners on and combed the teasing out of her hair. Through the walls, she heard the soundtrack of the movie rising in pitch.

It was dusk. The streetlights were flickering. Lilah felt a surge of triumph. She wouldn't have to call her father for a ride. No difficult explanations—just this experience and now home. It wasn't so bad doing a thing alone.

On the sidewalk, Lilah kept her head bowed and hoped that no one would drive by and recognize her in a dress and running shoes. She imagined Mr. Sherman driving past and spotting her. Somehow, things would shift—he would be the one in control then. It was important to go on fooling him.

As she walked, Lilah began to feel a bit sick at the reckless thing she had just done—at the idea of losing Suzette and not being able to visit her again at the house on the lake. She wondered at herself doing a thing like this to someone who was supposed to be her best friend. But Suzette would handle the situation. She was becoming very skilled.

Lilah wondered what the two men would do. She pictured the way they would try not to look at each other.

She heard the running footsteps but didn't have time to whirl before a thump landed on her back. Speechless, mortified, Lilah spun and faced Suzette. Some colour had come back into Suzette's face, and she was grinning as if events had gone exactly as planned.

"Why didn't you give me a signal that you were making the getaway! Let's beat it before they're on to us."

"I didn't know that you'd want to—" Lilah stuttered.

She wondered if Suzette had misunderstood, or not seen how she had been abandoned. Or maybe the rules of allegiance shifted when men were involved. Lilah struggled to say something that would save their friendship after all, and then stopped, seeing that it wasn't necessary to explain herself or to apologize. Suzette was already running ahead, her high heels clicking hard and rhythmically down the sidewalk.

A Trip For One

Mac tapped his pipe against the barn door and watched the ashes fall to the ground. Reaching into his shirt pocket, he took out a fresh clump of tobacco and stuffed it into the bowl. The smoke swirled behind him as he crossed the yard to look out over the fields. Eleanor had been gone for more than two hours. She must have left the ranch to ride along the road.

Resting his elbows on the fence, Mac puffed slowly on his pipe. The woods at the end of the pasture waved in a solid, sultry motion in the wind. Beyond them, the drumlins reminded him of Exmoor when he was ten years old and riding his pony in local hunts—the only son in a family of daughters, the apple of everyone's eye. Mac looked away from the distant hills.

He wiped the back of his hand across his forehead. The wind might be blowing in rain. He studied the trees below, wishing the foliage would part like a curtain and reveal Eleanor and his horse as they emerged from the woods. It made him nervous to have her gone this long. There had been some close calls over the past year. Once, when she had been galloping the horse around the track, Galahad had shied at something and Eleanor had hurtled through the air, brushing across the top of a post. When Mac raced to her side and pulled up her shirt, her stomach looked as if it had been combed with something sharp—tiny beads of blood forming in rows.

Another time, her foot had been caught in the stirrup when she tried to dismount. Instead of bolting, Galahad had demonstrated his police-horse training by stopping. Mac had felt proud of his horse that night. Still, it could be a dangerous sport, and she was just a kid, a novice. She knew that he liked her to check in regularly.

I'll give her what-for when she gets back, Mac thought. Something painful throbbed in his right temple. He sucked in his breath and let the air out in a long angry whistle. I won't call her for a few nights, teach her a lesson.

Being invisible for a stretch might be wise anyway. He sensed that Eleanor's parents were disenchanted with him. Her mother sounded abrupt the last time he called to say he'd be taking Eleanor to the ranch.

At first the woman had been all agog over him, especially when he came around in his uniform. They remembered that he and Nadine had rented the Johnston's upstairs apartment years earlier. They were sympathetic about his divorce, impressed when he told them that he was writing a book of short stories. And wasn't it great that Eleanor had a horse to ride. They even asked him about various laws, treating him like a lawyer, a professional. But suddenly they seemed to think less of him. The police chief had approached him about a few things. Maybe the rumours were filtering through town now; maybe Eleanor's mother had heard one of them.

Mac watched Van Felt's horses grazing in the field—thoroughbreds, quarter horses, two Arabians. Van Felt had invested too much too fast; he was in over his head. Still Mac could sympathize with the desire to own horses like these and be the overseer of a large ranch. Horses always gave him the same feeling of power, richness, beauty. He regretted not riding much anymore. Too much weight and a hint of arthritis. The best days of his life had been when he and Nadine were newly married, newly emigrated, and he was riding Galahad on the police beat through the parks along the edge of Lake Ontario. At least he was getting a kick out of teaching Eleanor how to groom Galahad, how to lift the horse's hooves and clean out the day's accumulation of dirt and grass, how to polish the leather saddle.

He had a dim memory of seeing Eleanor when she was about eight—a thin, pale girl playing with a hula hoop on the front lawn of the house where he and Nadine were renting the top floor. They had been through another wild one that afternoon—he had hit her again. Not caring that the Johnstons were listening in their living room downstairs, Mac had slammed the bedroom door and stood by a hall window that overlooked the lawn. The neighbourhood kids were down there, making exaggerated motions to spin the hoops around their waists. His eyes had fallen on Eleanor's clear, open face and silky brown hair.

Funny that he had crossed paths with her again after six years. He believed in the significance of such coincidences.

He had always loved kids. Nadine hadn't wanted to get pregnant. She hadn't wanted to do much of anything towards the end.

As Mac began to walk toward the barn, his face tightened into a frown. Now that he was facing south, he could see that a storm was definitely moving in. If Eleanor were much longer, he'd have to go and hunt for her. You'll see me coming and know you're in for it, Mac muttered out loud.

She had mentioned something once about members of a motorcycle gang living at the foot of the hill. "Someone told me that Satan's Choice live along here," she had said to Mac one morning as they drove up the gravel road.

She had stopped abruptly to stare at the woods they were passing—as if she were looking for something. Mac had glanced at the silver birch and ironweed trees and then at the row of small wooden houses they were passing. A boy with long hair and a suede coat with fringes was standing on one of the lawns. The lawn was a mess of truck tires, toys, and dandelions. The hippies had bought up these shacks the past few years.

"Just a story at school," Eleanor had said quickly. "Somebody must have been teasing me."

"Maybe you shouldn't ride down here. What's the matter with the track where I'm handy if something happens?"

"Galahad could outrun any of them. Anyway, they'd never try anything—not in daylight."

"Well, don't worry about it."

"I wouldn't be scared," Eleanor had announced.

"Nothing scares you, right?" Mac had grinned at her in a challenging, meaningful way. He swerved the car to tease her, to make her slide across the seat up against him. "You just tell them your old man is a cop; they'll leave you alone."

"Old man? You?"

"I'm putting you on!" He reached over to nudge her. He felt irritated that she had missed his joke.

She had been silent for a second. Then, she smiled at him and tossed her head. "I know."

It always surprised him when she spoke as if she were an adult. It was one of the things that drew him to her. She had the quickness, the ability to adopt the reaction—a womanly one—that he expected of her.

Mac stopped in the yard and gazed at nothing, thinking. If she was riding along the road and she believed the bikers were there. . . . He laughed aloud at his own thoughts. He had checked some files at the station and, although one or two bikers had lived around here a few years ago, there was no record of that now. Anyway, Eleanor wasn't a girl who'd set out to tempt fate. Mac grinned. Sometimes, he wished she would be a little slyer.

At first, meeting her here at Van Felt's ranch a year ago, he had thought of her as a niece, even as a daughter. Her father had been with her, cautious and watchful, trying to find a place for Eleanor to do some riding. After a few weeks, Mac realized the girl was slipping into his thoughts, his daydreams. She had a way of moving, of grooming the horse and putting him through his paces, that was unstudied yet graceful. Mac fantasized about having her turn sixteen. He liked the idea of being her mentor, a Svengali. There were plenty of instances throughout history of relationships like that. Ageing kings and their very young brides—so young that sometimes consummation of the marriage had to be postponed. He had even tried to write a story about that—about marrying a girl as young as Eleanor, sweeping her off to a lavish honeymoon in England, guiding her through the landmarks of his boyhood.

His Oldsmobile was parked beside the hay bin. On his way past, Mac noticed that Eleanor's side hadn't been locked. He opened the car door to check the glove compartment. On the passenger seat, in a bed of tissue, lay the mirror, brush and comb set. The mirror had a quilted yellow satin back.

"Thank you," Eleanor had breathed when she unwrapped his gift on the way out this morning. "They're beautiful."

Training his gaze straight ahead along the gravel road, he had sensed something unusual: She didn't know what else to say. She was embarrassed. She had run the comb through her hair with an air of reluctance. And the whole time, she had looked out the window at the passing farms. He couldn't understand what had gotten into her: he knew that she liked the gift. He didn't understand why she had flinched like that, drawn back.

He almost regretted buying her the comb set. At first, his surprises had pleased her. In the spring, he had gone to Police School in Aylmer for a two-week conference. During his absence, he wrote her letters. When he returned, he brought her a pair of riding boots, jodhpurs, and a hard hat. "If she's going to ride my thoroughbred, she's going to have to look the part," he joked with her parents. Everyone was pleased. For her birthday, he bought a pink jewelry box that had velvet compartments for bracelets. On a small mirror, a miniature ballerina with dark hair and a white lace costume twirled as long as the box was open.

Eleanor had asked him once, "Did you buy your wife presents?"

"Now and then."

"Why did your wife want to go back to England?"

"Who knows. I hear she's shacked up with some guy over there. He can have her—all she did was bitch and cry. Whew! Could she fight!" Mac laughed. Sometimes, he got the feeling that she used Nadine as a topic of conversation. She used it to steer him away from talking about other things.

Occasionally, he saw Eleanor when he was doing the sidewalk beat downtown with another officer. She never came near him. She knew not to. He wondered what he would do if she ever approached him downtown. The way pressure was mounting at headquarters these days, it could be awkward if he was observed. Once, she and two of her girlfriends walked past him at the four corners. He had felt disconnected—as if she belonged to a different universe, a different life altogether. He realized he felt jealous, possessive of her—the way he had over girls in his single days.

Mac kept his pistol in the glove compartment on days off. Peering inside, he lifted out maps, a pair of sunglasses, and a package of Chiclets to uncover the gun. He checked the chambers and stroked the polished black handle. Looks as if I may be turning you in soon, he muttered. The throbbing in his temple began to ache again.

107

He set the gun down and ran his finger over the yellow satin back of the mirror. He turned it over suddenly to reflect his face. He studied his mouth, then his eyes. He wondered what was in his face that he himself couldn't see. Men he had worked alongside for years—fellow officers that he counted on as friends—had been filing complaints about him. Reports had been written.

"The biggest damned frame since Mona Lisa," Mac said aloud.

He rubbed his finger across his chin and stared at his reflection. His lips were still as red as they had been when he was a boy, and his teeth were very small.

Replacing the gun in the glove compartment, Mac slammed the car door and leaned over to glance at himself in the side mirror. His hair hadn't started to grey yet; but his face was deepening, falling into lines and looseness. He straightened and stepped back to look at his car, admiring the wax job. It had been an impulsive buy, this car—but owning a powerful vehicle made him feel good.

He began to walk back into the gloom of the barn, thinking. If the force let him go, he wouldn't have many options—not at forty-four. He could go back to England. Nadine had gone back five years ago. He hated to think of the satisfaction it would give her to hear that he was jobless, crawling back. He'd lie of course. Couldn't stand one more Canadian winter. . . . But what about his car? Galahad? Eleanor?

In the airy arena that separated the stalls from the feed and tack rooms, a group of regulars were gathered around the Coke machine. Mac walked toward them. One day, they were friendly and the next, they weren't. He knew they raised their eyebrows and speculated now that he was coming to the barn with Eleanor. It entertained him to keep them guessing, wondering what it was that attracted a young girl like Eleanor who could

108

easily spend her time with boys her own age if she wanted to. It was the kind of thing people laughed about, but were secretly enthralled by.

One of the group, Van Felt, the red-faced, hard-bodied man who owned the ranch, turned to face Mac. "Good morning." He put his hand out.

Mac shook it, bemused. Normally, Van Felt muttered and turned his head away when he saw Mac.

"I got a legal question to ask you."

Mac looked at the squinting, dusty face of the rancher. He reached into his pocket and began to refill his pipe. "That so?"

"Someone's trying to sue me over the second mortgage I took on this place," Van Felt told him. "I wondered if you could stall things for a while—till I get hold of some money. Provincial Police may be here this weekend to serve me a summons. Maybe not." The rancher shrugged his shoulders and grinned.

Mac felt everyone watching him. A sensation he had almost forgotten, of pride and importance, swelled in his chest. "I'll be over to the house to use your phone in a while—I'll talk about it then if you want; maybe we can work out an arrangement."

He winked at the others and walked away, feeling pleased. That would change their tune for a while. He felt a sudden camaraderie with Van Felt. He knew what it was like to be in trouble where debts were concerned.

In the tack room, Mac took down one of Galahad's bridles, a tin of polish, and a rag, aromatic and black from use. Sitting on the bench, he began to polish the chin strap and reins of the bridle. His pipe had gone out so he removed it from his mouth and set it on the overturned crate beside him. He heard a pinging noise overhead and realized the rain had started. His head grew warm with a slow anger. Where the hell was she? He tried to think about something else—his writing, a collection of his stories that he planned to call "A Trip for One." He was almost finished a piece about a married woman who was followed home by a large, handsome, but menacing, stranger who turned out to be her long-lost brother-in-law, Mac himself.

The group of regulars had moved further down the arena to the tuck shop where Van Felt stocked bags of chips and peanuts. Their laughter was shrill and penetrating. It'd never cross their minds to invite Mac to join them. He put his weight into the task of polishing the bridle's leather straps.

He began to think about an incident a week earlier that kept rankling him. He had been leaning against the gatepost one afternoon when Eleanor galloped up from the woods, her shoulder-length, light brown hair moving like a flag in the wind. He had watched her landing rhythmically against the saddle. When she slowed to a trot and began to post, he thought she pressed herself against the leather saddle longer than she had to.

She stopped Galahad near the gate, and Mac tapped his pipe against the fence, looking at her closely.

"Are you wearing a bra?"

She laughed lightly. "Of course I am."

He continued, winking at her. "The way you were bouncing out there, I wouldn't have bet on it."

"Why do you call it 'braaa'?"

"How do you pronounce it?"

Instead of answering, she turned her head away.

"So you like Galahad and me," Mac said, drawing his arm up and around his horse's neck.

"I love him." Eleanor leaned forward along the saddle to encircle the horse's thick neck with her arms. She looked at Mac through the wisps of mane veiling her face and smiled. "I do love him," she said, burying her face in the horse's hair.

Mac grinned. She means me, he thought. "And you like riding him, don't you?"

110

"You know I do." She had looked over her shoulder at the woods.

"But why do you like to ride?"

She looked squarely at him, her head tilted, and shrugged. "I just like it."

She had been warm in her offhand girlish fashion on the way home. He had pulled her across the seat and let her drive, leaning against him, her arms stretched across his chest to steer the wheel of the big Olds—a sport that he knew entertained her. Her shoulder and thigh had felt firm and warm against his own. He had his arm around her, his hand dangling, occasionally brushing up against her breast. Each time he accelerated, she laughed loudly, excitedly.

"I want you to see my place tonight," Mac had told her.

She slid over to her side of the car again. "You want me to see it," she repeated.

He lived in a high-rise on the outskirts of town. They took an elevator to the 14th floor and Mac let Eleanor walk ahead of him into the apartment before switching the light on behind her. He had been dizzy with anticipation. He had been entertaining a vague dream, a dim picture of what might take place.

He owned hardly any furniture—an enormous television, a couch, coffee table, regulation drapery. The furnishings of a man without a woman. He had showed her the first room and then his office—a writing desk, brass floor lamp, and a reclining chair.

"My reading chair," he had said. "Want to try it out?"

She sat on the edge, her feet dangling. He stood over her, waiting for her to lie back, trying to will her to lie down just by standing over her. But she kept her head bowed. He had been tempted to touch her shoulder—a little pressure to start her moving backward.

"How would you like to hear one of my stories?

You just sit there and I'll read it to you."

He read her a clever, amusing story about a man who brought "her" home, shapely and smooth; caressed and admired "her"—and then announced in the last sentence that "she" was a "damned fine bottle of scotch!" When he finished, Mac looked up, grinning, and Eleanor laughed and clapped her hands and looked down at her lap again.

He crossed the room to his desk to take out a book he had bought for her, *The World of Horses.*

"These are really nice pictures," she said.

A reproachful and expectant silence filled the room—just the sound of Eleanor flipping pages and studying the photographs, stalling. Mac remained standing beside the reclining chair. Every few pages, she uttered a sigh or a remark about a picture. She turned over the final page slowly and then firmly shut the book.

"Wow, thank you." She looked up at him then with an expression on her face that he hadn't seen before: pleading, hopeful, miserable. It had occurred to him that she was going along with things to please him. He was frightening her. He had felt ashamed, impatient, furious. He had stared at her and she returned his gaze, but not with the gentle, seductive warmth he was used to in her. A look in her eye flickered—he couldn't put a name to it. Finally, he had stepped back. "Time to get you home, I guess."

He wasn't good at analyzing things; he couldn't really say what had happened that evening. His understanding of events tended to form without words. He wasn't stupid, he was sure—but he was deliberate. And it was in this wordless way that he felt things slipping—his life, career, marriage, pride, security. He had allowed people to trick him. Somehow, even Eleanor had tricked him.

She wants to ride the horse, that's all, he thought. He envied her suddenly—her youth, her spiritedness. She had something he lacked, something he wanted. He felt defeated imagining the possibilities that still lay ahead of her, the kind of woman she'd turn out to be.

He pressed the blackened cloth into the tin of polish and leaned over the bridle.

She must have learned something about him recently that he hadn't meant to reveal—or that he didn't even know about himself. Mac couldn't force his mind to shape things any more clearly than that. Without a doubt though, it had been a mistake taking her to the apartment. She had been unable to disguise her uneasiness. And she had been awkward about the brush and comb set today. Nothing like the possibilities he had imagined.

What I'd give for a good stiff shot of scotch right now, Mac thought. He wished he could leave the ranch and drive to his apartment, lie down on the reclining chair and have a scotch. Maybe call a woman he had met in a bar two weeks ago. But he had let too much time slip past; she had probably forgotten who he was. There was something about women his own age that left him cold now.

The rain was pelting the tin roof overhead. Mac threw the cloth back on the shelf and put the bridle over a nail in the wall. The arena was illuminated by lamps in the high ceiling. The light seemed too dim, as if the low-hanging, wet clouds had forced their way inside the barn. The rain slapped the tin roof.

My saddle is going to be ruined, he realized, looking out the open barn door to the yard where the earth, dried and gutted with hoofprints, was turning to mud again. He had paid too much for the English saddle in the first place, and now she was letting the rain soak it. He stopped and stared dully at a set of headlights that were pulling into the yard from the driveway. She wasn't riding at all—she was with somebody, in one of those

113

houses at the foot of the hill, or in the woods. She couldn't be riding in this downpour.

He looked up and saw Van Felt stride across the arena. The headlights in the yard switched off and a car door slammed. An OPP officer got out and started to walk toward the barn door where Van Felt was waiting, his legs astride, hands on his hips. Mac walked toward the entrance.

He grinned in a way that he knew was showing his respectability, his membership in this young guy's club. "Can we help you out? Mac Robertson. With the City Force." He extended his hand to the OPP officer. "And you are?"

The OPP officer took Mac's outstretched hand without answering and turned back to Van Felt. "I'm looking for the owner of this ranch—Hans Van Felt. He's defaulted on a second mortgage."

Van Felt crossed his arms. "He's left for the day—won't be back till the first of the week."

Mac saw from the corner of his eye that Eleanor had returned. A damp wind was still gusting through the barnyard. Hair blew in the girl's eyes as she dismounted and walked toward the crowd that had gathered in the yard by the open barn door.

Mac looked pointedly at his watch and then back at the OPP officer facing him—a young man, his chin rosy in places where the razor had scraped his skin. The officer dug the heel of his boot into the wet soil. He looked grimly at Mac who was still grinning, tapping his pipe into the palm of his hand. "It doesn't matter—I've got to serve this summons. If you'll just tell me where I can find the owner of this place," the officer said. He glanced at Eleanor and away.

"Look, I told you," Mac said. "I'm saving you valuable time. Why don't you just take the summons and head off? Come back in a week, maybe." He winked at the officer, who darkened perceptibly and ducked his head. "Now here's my horse and my girlfriend," Mac joked. "Just in time for dinner. Come on girl, we've got to get that saddle off before the rain gets worse."

Mac watched as Eleanor led Galahad down the arena to the stall. He saw her remove the wet saddle and blanket and walk quickly across the arena to deposit them in the tack room. The blanket was dripping. When he turned back, the OPP officer was heading in the direction of his cruiser.

In the open barn door, Van Felt shook Mac's hand.

"Thanks for covering up for me out there. And don't worry—I'll get things straightened out on Monday."

"You do that." Mac said. "Now, about our arrangement: let's say fifty bucks less a month for the stall?"

Van Felt screwed up his face and avoided looking at Mac. "That'll have to do," he said.

In Galahad's stall, Eleanor was working with the fork, rustling the straw and rearranging it the way Mac had taught her.

"Sorry," she said as Mac entered the stall. "It was raining so hard that I took cover under some trees." Mac took the pitchfork from her hands and in silence began to fork out the straw. She started to groom Galahad's broad, gleaming body, gently yanking the tangles from his mane and tail with a thick-bristled brush. She pulled the brush across his back and followed with her hand. Mac watched her standing behind the horse and putting her weight against his flanks, confident that he would never kick her.

"Let's go," he said.

In the car, Eleanor avoided catching his glances. He wondered how much she had overheard—and suddenly he saw what had taken place at the ranch as if he were looking through Eleanor's eyes, through her parents' eyes. He had made a fool of himself. A sick feeling rose in his throat. Before the day was over, that OPP guy would report what had taken place at the ranch: obstruction of justice—and by a fellow policeman.

Mac's fingers tightened on the leather cover of the wheel. A sudden, unbidden picture formed in his mind—the reports filed about his brutality with drunks who spent nights in the cell; and worse, the night last month when he touched a sixteen-year old girl where he shouldn't have. But she had been a little vixen, real jail-bait, in on a vagrancy charge. And now this afternoon's episode with the OPP. They'll have all the evidence they need to get me off the Force, he thought. Hands down. The heavy sensation, dark and leaden, settled in his body. He felt his face draining of blood.

Eleanor sat beside him on the front seat and drew her fingers through the silky bristles of the yellow brush.

It had stopped raining. The birch trees on both sides were vibrating and brilliant. Eleanor kept her eyes lowered.

As they approached the row of box-shaped houses along the road, a figure appeared at the edge of a lawn. Mac tapped his foot on the brake and the Oldsmobile slowed a little. A boy raised his hand half-way, a kind of salute or wave. Mac pressed the brake further. It was the kid with the fringed suede coat.

Eleanor cried out, "Don't stop—I don't want to talk to him." She stared at Mac.

"That your boyfriend?"

"No. I know him from school. I don't even like him," she added hastily.

"Have you been meeting him down here?"

"Sometimes I see him when I'm riding."

"That so?" Mac gave a laugh. His eyes jerked down to her legs and took in the jodhpurs, how soaked they were. Grass stains.

On the highway, he passed the diner where they

116

usually stopped for french fries. They both started to say something.

"I was going to ask you about the other policeman," Eleanor said. "Does it matter that he left the ranch so angry?"

Mac could hear her struggling to steady her voice, not to reveal how frightened she was. He muttered, "Not much." He looked out his window, although it was almost dark now and the glass was wet. His mind kept forming a picture of Eleanor kissing that baby-faced boy. Why hadn't he guessed that she was meeting someone in the woods?

He drummed his fingers on the steering wheel. "I hope you haven't done anything foolish with him."

"No," Eleanor replied lightly.

He heard the effort in her voice to conceal something, to have one over on him. I'm thirty years older than she is, Mac thought. He had made himself look unethical, ridiculous in front of that young cop. There was no one to blame but himself. I've botched my life. No time to start over.

He turned sharply and swung the Oldsmobile onto a different road.

Eleanor said breathily, "Where are we going?"

"Christ knows," Mac said. He gave a slight laugh and glanced down at the glove compartment. "I want to show you something—to prove how safe you always are with me."

He pulled over and flicked on the overhead car light. Unlatching the glove compartment, he fumbled for the gun in front of Eleanor's knees, keeping his eyes on her face. She stared at him, and at his hands, and then out the car window.

He pulled the gun out and balanced it in one palm in front of her.

"I'm leaving the City Force," he said. With his free hand, he slapped the steering wheel. "I won't be

117

around for you any longer. I wanted you to see this—to know about it. All the time we've been going out to ride, I've had this handy."

He stared down at the pistol and briefly imagined turning it on her, pressing against her pale, uncomplicated forehead and squeezing the trigger. But that was impossible. He couldn't begin to see it, to imagine it. He loved her. And he wasn't one to turn a gun on somebody. For a fleeting moment, he pictured turning the gun on himself.

"Where will you go?" she stammered.

"Now why would that matter to you?"

He studied the gun in his hand, his thumb curling over the handle, pressing it until he felt his wrist ache. He could do it: press the trigger and blast her head open. Stop her in her tracks. Save her from having to grow up. The unsettling ache in his gut twisted his lips into a thin smile. He looked up at Eleanor. Her skin was bleached white with fear. He could see her chest moving rapidly. His smile relaxed, widened. Alarm was forcing her to respect him. He had wanted to see that. He bounced the pistol in the palm of his hand and grinned at the girl.

He replaced his gun in the glove compartment and pressed the gas pedal until the engine was roaring. Putting the car into gear, he swung away from the shoulder and sped down the uneven, wet country road to town. He felt her distancing herself, pressing against the car door. He looked at the evening ahead of him, the tunnel of hours to put in by himself. He thought bleakly about his writing project, about the sheaf of blank pages lying on his writing desk. Maybe, it was time for a break—a holiday back to Cornwall. He could get some writing done there. Look up some old friends. He felt himself growing more relaxed, pleased with himself for having arrived at a solution so easily.

When the familiar homes and trees of Eleanor's neighbourhood came into view, Mac slowed down. He realized how much it had been bothering him to drive into this part of town for the past year. Without turning, he reached out and gave Eleanor one of his playful shoves.

"Will I see you next week?" she asked him in a soft, artificially high voice.

She was wearing that expression on her face again—forlorn, wistful. Relieved. He looked at her sharply, taken aback suddenly by the sympathy he saw in her eyes. She felt sorry for him. He didn't want her to leave the car yet. This wasn't how he wanted things to end. A movement in the kitchen window drew his attention—Eleanor's mother was leaning over, peering through the darkening night to his car.

"Goodnight," Mac said.

As Eleanor got out and shut his car door, fumbling with the brush set in her haste, he kept his eyes looking straight ahead into the backyard of her parent's property—a black, drenched expanse of grass and maple trees. He waited to see if she would stop to wave before going into the house, but she didn't. Looking over his shoulder, Mac backed the Oldsmobile out of the driveway and began to plan his trip back home.

The Candystriper

As Jill waits, she keeps her hands in the pockets of her uniform. In one, she can feel a pillbox that she stole from the gift shop last Saturday with Myra Landon. In the other pocket, she has a thermometer—and a wad of lab results which she now takes out to leaf through. She finds the one for Clara Marin and studies it. Often, she is able to figure out what the abbreviations and medical terminology mean.

Soon, the elevator doors will open and Myra will step off. Recently, it has occurred to Jill that people may wonder at a schoolgirl who volunteers in the wards nearly every day. She wants to look less absorbed, less intense; she likes Myra to join her so that the doctors and nurses see her with a friend now and then. There is a sultriness about Myra, something lazy and sensual. Jill imagines that people around the hospital remark what an attractive, seductive pair they are.

At the beginning of a shift, she always enters her name in the Candystriper Register, checks to see where she has been assigned, and then goes to the 6th floor to see if the pathologist is in his laboratory. Dr. Arnold is a large, stern-looking, bearded man, balding, with thick red hair curling down his arms to his white hands. A peculiar smell that may be formaldehyde lingers whenever he passes by. He never smiles. Jill supposes it is the work he does—an occupational hazard. In an elevator with him, or if her eyes lock with his through the open door while she is removing slips from wooden slots outside his laboratory, she freezes and flushes as pink as her uniform. He is strong-looking and handsome. His closeness to death fascinates her—that he can look at it and touch it with his hands and yet remain stern and reserved. She wonders if he sits across the dinner table from his wife at the end of each day and visualizes her forehead pulled back to reveal the bone, the brain beneath.

Underneath her uniform she wears bikini underwear with sayings such as "Kiddo," "I Love You," and "Eat Your Heart Out." She wears jewellery as well—silver-sequined watchbands and fortune-teller rings.

Like an explorer of uncharted territory, Jill keeps daring herself further into the recesses of the hospital. Two days ago she went into the surgeons' change room, aware that a doctor might suddenly emerge naked from a shower. While she was looking around, she came across an artificial body on a stretcher. The torso was lying open to reveal various plastic organs—presumably so that doctors could refresh their memories before going next door to cut a person open. And in Dr. Arnold's lab, when no one was there, Jill peered into a jar containing horrible, malodorous parts, and in one, a human embryo.

It gives her a shudder of delight to take risks. She likes to picture Dr. Arnold discovering her in his lab and the passionate scene that will result. She has not yet figured out what she will say if this happens.

"I'll know what to say when the time comes," she thinks.

A few doctors and nurses pass her in the corridor. A nurse nods and says, "How are you today?" Despite the fact that she wears a name tag, not many know her name, not even after two years. She is on the periphery of the real action.

Earlier this morning, Jill spent an hour with Clara,

who is sixty-two. Clara's test results, which Jill brings down from the 6th floor, have checkmarks alongside cancer boxes. Clara is peacefully waiting to die; she seems unfazed at having to do it alone.

This morning, Jill helped her to complete the week's menu request. Clara pressed the pencil gingerly into the paper and circled, "Roast Potato," and then added in a shaky, feminine script, "an extra pat of butter."

"If you ask them nicely, you often get what you want," she assured Jill.

"Will anyone from your family come this afternoon?" Jill asked her.

She lifted a comb from the bedside table and began to draw it through Clara's hair. This has become part of their routine. But this morning, a ball of soft grey hair that felt like kitten's fur came away from Clara's scalp.

"They'll do their best to get here," Clara smiled, her eyes closed. If she knew that her hair had just come away in a clump, she pretended not to.

Jill wanted to take the hair and pat it back into Clara's head, intertwine it with the hair still there. She wonders about Clara's family. She has never seen anyone visit the old lady, who always wears satin-blue bedjackets and lipstick as if she were expecting someone. Who will bury Clara? Who will her pall bearers be?

Pal bearers, Jill thought.

Occasionally, the old woman is curious to know what Jill studies at school and what she will do with her life in the way of a career.

"And do you have a boyfriend?" she asked this morning while Jill patted the comb against her hair.

"Yes. . .well, sometimes," Jill said reluctantly. "He plays guitar in a band that does songs by The Grateful Dead," she explained. "Maybe you haven't heard of the group. . . ." she trailed off when she saw the puzzled look in Clara's eyes.

She doesn't want to divulge much. Cliff is two

124

years older than Jill and in Grade 13. They have been dating for several years. He is dark and tends to stoop and look thinner than he is. He drinks Maalox from the bottle because of an ulcer. Right now, they are not seeing each other—except at school where it is unavoidable. He is angry again. Jill got drunk for the first time recently. She took off her blouse and threw it out the car window at a gas station where Cliff had stopped to fill his MG. At first, he laughed and went to retrieve it, but his amusement soured when the attendant took ten minutes to wash the windshield so that he could look at Jill who had passed out topless on the front seat. The next afternoon, while Jill was at school, Cliff went to her mother and described what happened. He pretends that he does things like this out of personal integrity.

Things have become hazy and uncertain since they started to have sex in a spare bed in his mother's basement. The sheets are always damp and cold. Jill has to cajole him to make love—usually by selecting unlikely places. One night at a party in a friend's house, she convinced Cliff to find a bedroom upstairs. Afterwards, she sat up on the bed beside him and looked through the window down the dark road to her own house where her parents were sleeping. Another time, she talked him into making love in a field near the park with Jill underneath. When they stood up, his back was covered with insect bites; and hers, scratched by the straw, sharp as a knife.

His mother's second husband—Cliff's father died on a motorcycle when Cliff was ten—came home one night to find Cliff having a party and two highschool friends in the damp bed downstairs.

"They fucking—they fucking in our cellar," his stepfather yelled in his thick, stupid-sounding foreign accent.

Cliff was so angry and humiliated that he did not call Jill for a week. He has a way of making her responsible, twisting things so that they can't be cleared up.

Jill doesn't want to talk about him to Clara. It is too embarrassing to describe things. He has hit Jill twice—most recently, late at night on a neighbour's lawn several blocks from home. He left her lying there, stunned, with the sensation of her heart being squeezed with hurt and disappointment till she couldn't think straight. He hasn't been like this from the start. It has taken a long time for her to become dependent on him and for him to become so hateful. There is no one she can talk about Cliff to—not even Myra who has become a friend.

"We're going to Midnight Mass together on Christmas Eve," Jill told Clara this morning.

"Won't that be marvellous," Clara replied.

"It really will," Jill said, thinking of standing alongside Cliff in the warm candle-lit church and singing carols with the wintry night outside approaching Christmas day.

Clara doesn't have much in the way of decor. Many of the long-term patients make an apartment of their hospital rooms. They attach prints to the wall, usually the colourful, messy finger-paintings of a niece or nephew. And everyone has daisies and chrysanthemums. But, Clara has only a few get-well cards, a box of chocolates and two library books.

"I have to get going—my friend arrives soon. I'll see you again tomorrow," Jill promised as she left this morning.

Clara smiled. "You must have to study for Christmas exams."

Jill stopped in the doorway. She tried not to stare at the ball of white hair on the floor beneath Clara's bed. "I never have trouble with exams. It doesn't matter if it's Christmas," she said.

She had the sense again of how unusual she must appear to people, how solitary, mysterious, on the outside of things. She has already decided that she will come in on Christmas Day.

126

"If Myra doesn't show up soon, I'll go back to see if Clara needs anything from the gift shop," she thinks. It will be advantageous to be seen purchasing something for a patient.

Jill catches her breath as Dr. Arnold walks through the foyer. There is something aristocratic in his casualness, a grace in his tall, healthy presence. His eyes flicker to where Jill is sitting on the sofa. She feels herself lose control of the expression on her face.

She watches him continue along the corridor and push open the swinging doors that lead into the new wing of the hospital. Is she mistaken or is he studying Jill seated behind him as her reflection flashes in the window of the door? The thought that he might want to catch her observing him makes her flush.

She remembers something that took place when her father picked her up from the hospital on his way to work one evening. She has been learning to drive and was at the wheel when she saw Dr. Arnold through the car window, walking home along a city sidewalk. Her thoughts froze at seeing the man on the city street, out of his clinical white smock. She was so distracted, she took her father's car out of their lane, across the centre line and into the approaching lane of cars.

"Where do you think you're going?" her father said disbelievingly.

"Oh," Jill said, swerving back into place.

But Dr. Arnold whirled as an oncoming car honked, and he saw her. She is sure of it.

"But did he see that we were almost in an accident because I was watching him?" Jill wonders.

The pathologist disappears down the corridor on the other side of the door, his bald head bobbing. Of all the doctors she admires and follows about, Dr. Arnold figures most prominently in her dreams. She likes to imagine scenes in which she is struck by a car and rushed, minimally injured, to Emergency where Dr. Arnold will carry her from the stretcher into one of the treatment rooms to undress her. This event will lead to love. He will leave his wife—someone Jill envisions in tartan skirts and wool sweaters. Sometimes, she reverses things so that he is the one stricken and bedridden, and she, the hovering angel of mercy.

It is now 11:30 and Jill is beginning to feel hungry. Myra must have been out late the night before. It's worth waiting a few more minutes. There is a fearlessness about Myra Landon that Jill envies—a placid, smart, mocking sense of herself. In the introductory candystriper's class where they met, Myra was dressed like no one else—in a leopard-patterned vest and tight black skirt with a split. She has long dark hair like Jill's—in fact, they resemble each other. They are both pale. People ask if they are sisters.

Myra's boyfriend, Earl Rundle, is the son of a wealthy family who owns a funeral parlour. He is quiet and considerate of Myra. He doesn't try very hard at school because he will simply take over his father's business someday. Myra has his car to drive whenever she likes. She makes jokes about the cadavers in the Rundle Funeral home.

"You know where they put those tubes after you're dead, don't you? If you're a woman, you better watch those tubes. They push them right up you-know-where: right up through your mouth, from one end to the other," she likes to tell Jill.

Neither of them enjoys spending an entire shift on one ward. And each Saturday, they go to the gift shop. A month ago, Jill lifted a necklace off the counter and slipped it into her pocket. She showed the necklace to Cliff one night.

"I told my mother that you bought it for me—she'll get mad if I told her that I splurged on myself."

"I'll tell you what," Cliff said. "You give me the receipt and I will buy it for you—for Christmas. That

128

way, you won't have lied to your mother and I'll have given you something that you like."

She was taken by surprise at his craftiness. She knows that he was testing her. But she has been able to come up with a phoney receipt and produced it for him, knowing that he'll never give her the $40 for it. Now she is only taking smaller things—items like the pillbox in her pocket.

Myra is a good partner; she too likes to go where it is offbounds. On the surgery floor one Saturday morning, they watched through the window of the operating theatre while a patient underwent eye surgery. On the maternity ward, they left swiftly when they could hear a woman moaning as if she were being tortured, and sharp panicky cries coming from another room further along.

It seems unfair that love results in something so hard. Still it is something that everyone does. Cliff's mother, a large bossy woman, gave birth a year ago to a daughter by her new husband. She did not like being pregnant again and let everyone know it. The larger she got, the more sour Cliff became. On the day that she gave birth Jill and Cliff skipped school and went to sit by the creek at the park.

She took his hand and said, "Maybe we'll have a little Cliff someday." The words sounded weak and untrue to her own ears.

Cliff didn't challenge her. He stared into the water and said darkly, "Maybe."

As soon as she said it, Jill thought, What a lie.

They started to play-wrestle on the grass until a man emerged from a house overlooking the park and told them, "Go into the woods, why don't you? We've got two little kids and they're watching you." That time, Cliff didn't call her for two weeks.

Jill glances at her watch. She stands up and walks through the ward. The orthopedic patients are here—people who have been involved in car accidents and near-fatal mishaps. She hates to look through an open door and see them trussed up with ropes and pulleys, their bodies frozen in plaster. Any amount of confinement terrifies her. She often thinks she could go mad if forced to remain sitting or lying in one position for long.

Jill walks to the end of the corridor where a window overlooks the city. Through the window, she can see across the street to a palatial estate which has countless windows and chimney stacks. Everything is white with winter. In the middle of the enormous garden is a small building with an angel mounted on its roof. Jill wonders whether the wealthy man and his family are buried there. She stares at the sculptured, snow-covered fountain in the yard, and the need to absorb the sight and to preserve things in her memory fills her with a frantic sense of timing—of the shortness of things.

She feels sure that the two women in Admitting will report her absence. Twice now, the Coordinator of the candystipers has called Jill in about the way she wanders about the hospital without paying attention to the ward she is assigned to. It will be a matter of ducking the Coordinator over the next week.

I'm not a paid employee; this isn't a real job, Jill keeps thinking.

One of the women who works in Admitting is a short, plump, red-faced person who has a rolling, easy jolliness, quick to turn to sarcasm or disapprobation. The second woman is a spinster—Miss someone, tall and straight-backed with strained old-lady's legs cloaked in brown leotards.

Once an emergency came in—a woman had tried to kill herself and was screaming for her mother. The Miss from Admitting asked Jill to help wheel the woman's stretcher. As the woman screamed, Jill felt tears flood into her nose and throat. She glanced across the stretcher at the Miss and saw how amused she was. After they had left the stretcher in an examining room, Jill walked through a watery fog in time to collapse on a washroom floor.

Another time, a man was brought in from Lindsay, his face bruised purple, his eyes squeezed shut and surrounded by coarse black stitches, and two pegs in his jaw like Frankenstein's bolts. Jill was sick that day as well—not because of the injuries but because of the drama, the terror of possibilities in a person's life.

She likes to work in Admitting except that the two women make her feel obliged to show up. She doesn't want to suffer any instructions. But she likes to watch people bring their private lives, even their deaths, to the hospital. People come in with every problem imaginable. Often, if she hears a siren or the operator announcing "99..99," which means that someone's heart has stopped, Jill races to Emergency to witness the drama. It is a moving, reassuring sight to see the normally laconic nurses and arrogant doctors put themselves out to save someone's life.

The elevator door rings and Jill sees Myra emerging into the sunny area of the waiting room.

"Sorry I'm late. I was up till three," Myra says, grinning suggestively as Jill comes down the hall to meet her.

"What do you want to do first?" Jill asks her.

Myra looks at her watch. "It's noon. Do you want to go and have tea and donuts?"

"Let's."

The cafeteria is crowded. A few other candystripers are at a table talking—boring girls, predictable, obedient. Jill and Myra sit at a table by the window. Myra smokes while she eats her donut. She looks more pale than usual.

"I wonder if she really is sick," Jill thinks, recalling a mother-and-daughter dinner in September at which each girl received a cheap bracelet and a dime-sized charm with the number of hours served engraved on it. On the way home, Jill's mother said that Mrs.

Landon was concerned about Myra's health.

"I talked to her when you two were up on the stage and she said that Myra has been in Toronto for bone marrow tests. And you know what that means. That's a test for leukemia—cancer of the blood."

"But Myra's quite energetic," Jill protested.

"Mrs. Landon says that Myra is sluggish a lot of the time; she's ungodly pale," her mother added.

Jill feels almost jealous at the thought of Myra's dying an untimely, romantic death—and of the doctors that will hover about her bed. But she knows that Myra is pale because she smokes dope and stays up on week-nights till all hours with Earl.

They talk about Earl and Cliff—about sex and where they did it the first time. Myra's was in a hearse that belonged to her future father-in-law. Jill's was in the basement bed. They discuss whether it hurt much and what they are using. Jill is using withdrawal. Somehow, she has remained unpregnant. Her mother has threatened for years that if Jill ever becomes pregnant before getting married, she will jump off the harbour into Lake Ontario with Jill tied to her. A girl at school who is in Grade 12 is pregnant. Her mother is making her attend classes until the very last moment. The girl slides along the lockers and smiles foolishly. The boy who is the father has adopted a cool swagger and a new girlfriend. He is a friend of Cliff's. Each month, Jill waits, terrified to the point of numbness, for her period to begin.

Myra and Earl are using condoms. Myra carries several safes and a few joints in her purse.

With their hands in their pockets, they leave the cafeteria. As they begin to walk down the hall, Jill sees Dr. Arnold entering the servery. The sense of loss is overwhelming. She has missed an opportunity to have him see her. She ducks her head so that Myra won't see her reaction.

They go to the gift shop. The clerk is out back in the

stockroom. In the display case, they look through the glass at the ornamental cigarette cases, purse-sized ash-trays with pearl handles, pill-box, compacts with jew-elled lids. Jill watches as Myra pockets a red leather manicure set, so tiny it fits inside her palm. A row of key chains is on a rack—each one containing a bright new penny, dime or quarter. Jill fingers a key chain and slips it into her pocket. At that moment, the woman who runs the shop each Saturday emerges quietly and swiftly from the storeroom. Jill freezes, certain that the woman has seen her take the chain.

"Good morning," Myra says.

The woman frowns and Jill feels her heart skip a beat.

Is she going to make us turn our pockets out? she thinks desperately.

But the woman simply stares at them, not saying a word.

On their way to the geriatrics ward to make beds, they try to figure out whether the clerk is on to them.

"I think she knows. We shouldn't let her see us in there for a while," Jill says firmly. "If we were caught, the entire hospital would hear about it within an hour," she tells Myra.

She falters, alarmed at the truth in what she has just said.

On 6E, the old people's trays of lunch are arriving from the kitchen, smelling like tin and onions. Taking them from the carts, Jill and Myra carry the trays in to the patients.

Jill watches one of her favourite nurses move about the four-bed room. She is older than most of the nurses, grey-haired and with the limping gait of someone who has suffered illness herself. The nurse smiles and hums as she straightens the patients' beds. She talks to each one as she works, although the majority of these people are beyond conversation. Jill watches as she lifts the flaccid arm of an old woman to apply some deodorant.

Myra has sat down in a chair beside a patient whose name is Mrs. Gray. She begins to uncover the tin bowls on the tray to reveal some consommé soup, a plate of beef bourguignon, carrot cake, crackers for the soup. Jill sits in the chair opposite and tries not to look at the old woman's twisted feet.

They'll never be used for walking again, she thinks. She feels her stomach flip the way it did the morning the man from Lindsay came in.

She focusses on Myra, who has lifted a fork from the tray and is now cutting a corner from the carrot cake. She pops it into her mouth, lays the fork down, and begins to chew slowly, staring at the silent, mindless patient as she eats. Jill feels a thrill run up her spine. She forgets about the deformed feet.

"That's right—make her eat it up, girls," the nurse says behind them. "She doesn't know anymore that she's got to—just like a baby. Worse, actually. You make sure she eats every bit of that lunch."

"We'll do that," Myra says sweetly, swallowing the carrot cake and bowing her head as she flashes a look through her eyelashes at Jill.

As the nurse turns, Myra leans over and tears open the cellophane packet of soda biscuits. She crumbles three into the soup and eats one herself. "Now you eat that soup, Mrs. Gray," she says.

Mrs. Gray opens her mouth and a thin, silvery line of saliva rolls down her chin. Jill looks away and her eyes land on the old woman's feet.

"We've got to get going—we're supposed to be working in Admitting," she says to the nurse.

"I'll take over; you girls run along," the woman says.

Fortunately, Myra does not complain—or ask why Jill has suddenly gotten up to leave. Jill feels herself wrestling with nausea.

"I love children," Myra says as she and Jill walk through the pediatrics ward.

Jill has met girls like this before. She knows that wanting to be around kids has to do with pleasing other people—boyfriends and parents. It is a political thing to say, "I like children."

Jill glances at Myra. She feels jealous of Myra's relationship with Earl; it isn't fraught with anger and confusion. But there is something stultifying in having it all settled so soon. Still Myra is lucky. Earl would never hit her—he is too nice for that. He often drives Myra to the hospital to work as a candystriper and then picks her up three hours later. He likes his life to be intertwined with hers.

They are passing Clara's room.

I'll introduce Myra to Clara,ss Jill thinks.

It will take up some time in an afternoon which is turning out to feel long and tedious—something Jill resents. She never becomes restless candystriping alone, but she feels somehow responsible for Myra.

"Come in here for a minute," she says, tugging at Myra's sleeve.

Clara is sitting up in her chair, eating her lunch. She has finished the soup and is slowly working at the beef. She sets down her fork and knife, and pats her lips with a serviette as the girls come into the room.

"Hello again—you've brought your friend this time," Clara says, smiling.

In a tumbling flash, Jill knows she has made a mistake. Myra will say the wrong thing or offend Clara with her sultry, bored manner. She gropes for a reason to leave. The clump of hair is still visible beneath the bed. Jill watches, chilled, as Myra says hello and lifts the lid off the box of chocolates lying on the bedside table.

"May I?" she says, not looking at Clara, but at the candies.

Don't you realize that Clara isn't senile? Jill thinks.

"You go right ahead and have whatever you like," Clara says politely. She does not resume eating but sits very straight in her bed, smiling, and watching Myra who presses a chocolate and then giggling, replaces it and selects another.

Jill trembles with apprehension. "I think we should leave Clara to her lunch and come back later," she says.

"Whatever. . ." Myra comments. She has taken a second candy and her cheeks are jowled with chocolate.

Clara looks at Jill and nods her head, but Jill can see she is surprised—and there is something else: a wariness, the look of someone who believes she has misjudged.

When they leave Clara's room, Jill can't stop trembling. A sensation of regret and shame keeps rising in her throat, as it would if she pressed the gas pedal and ran over a small animal.

I'll just never visit Clara again, she thinks. Then she changes her mind. I'm blowing it out of proportion.

Thinking that, the pressure in her throat eases a bit. But she can't keep herself from glaring sideways at Myra who is walking and humming, oblivious to Jill's change of heart.

I think it's time you went home, Jill wants to say. But it's absurd—the hospital doesn't belong to her, and Myra will be shocked by such an attack.

"Let's go into the basement and smoke a joint," Myra says. She stops and faces Jill. "Or maybe I'll get going—I'm invited to Earl's parents for dinner," she says.

"Lucky you—I've never been invited to Cliff's place—not that I'd want to go," Jill adds, thinking of Cliff's stepfather and his resentful, dumb foreignness.

"You deserve someone better," Myra says. "Give him the boot. You should get a man, not a boy. How about one of these doctors?"

Jill flushes. She looks down the hall. Something

makes her feel dangerously close to tears.

"I'll talk to you in a week." Myra smiles. "Take this for the afternoon," she says, taking a fat-looking marijuana joint from her pocket and handing it to Jill. She waves over her shoulder and starts to walk away.

"Next Saturday is Christmas Day," Jill says, standing still and watching as Myra walks away.

"Sometime in January then—I'll call you," Myra waves.

No you won't, Jill thinks. She watches Myra disappear down the corridor and then turns to walk through the main foyer of the hospital. I'll go back to the geriatrics ward and help that nurse, she thinks.

She realizes someone has called her name several times before the voice cuts through her consciousness. Whirling, she see Cliff rise from a chair in the lobby. He is wearing a dark burgundy corduroy jacket that she always admires on him. He looks tall, wind-blown and handsome; but the darkness, the sardonic, defeating anger that eats away at him, gleams in his eyes.

"Where's the cafeteria—I want a coffee. I'm freezing," he says.

"What are you doing here?" she says, leading him down the hall to the cafeteria which is now almost empty.

"Don't you want me here?" He stops walking.

"Of course I do."

She realizes how many times over the past two years she has wanted him to come to meet her at the hospital so that she can show off the people she knows and how good she looks in her uniform. She has always wanted to share some of the wonder and mystery of the place.

"There are whole areas of my life that you don't know about," she thinks, standing behind him in the lineup.

They get themselves cups of coffee and sit at a table by the window. Jill feels suddenly foolish in her pink-

and-white striped uniform.

Thank God the cafeteria is empty, she hears herself thinking. She feels relieved that Dr. Arnold is not present to see her with Cliff who is scowling and unhappy-looking.

He reaches his hand into his pocket and takes out two twenty dollar bills. "There, take it. Now I've kept my promise. I'm taking off tonight with the band. We're going to Deerhurst to play on Christmas Eve."

"But we're supposed to go to Midnight Mass on Christmas Eve," Jill says helplessly.

She wonders if there is any way of warding off the inevitable fight. She has bought him a lighter and a leather tie for Christmas. Maybe the store will take them back. I can just go along with him, she thinks. I can pretend I don't mind.

"You should go with someone else. Why do you always have to have me with you?" Cliff says, sneering at her. He crosses his arms and looks out the window to the snow falling.

Jill looks across the table at him and then out the window in time to see Myra driving Earl's car out of the parking lot.

How am I going to give you up? she thinks, looking across the table again at Cliff. He is the person he is going to be forever; it will take incredible shocks and events to alter him. She hasn't been able to get what she wants—the thing that seems to come easily to other people.

She looks at him closely.

You don't make an effort—you don't love me enough to try, she thinks.

She wonders how Myra would handle a scene like this. I've got to stop dreaming, Jill tells herself. A surprising feeling of calmness enters her.

She folds the two bills into a neat rectangle and presses them into Cliff's hand. "I can't take the money from you."

"Why not?" he says suspiciously, his eyes narrowing.

"I can't tell you." It feels satisfying to have a secret—to be the one to hold something back. "And I've got to get going—I have to see a patient," Jill says. She stands up, pushes her chair in, and leaves the cafeteria without looking back.

As she walks along the hall to the elevator, something her mother has said comes back: "You can't admit he doesn't love you."

Jill wonders how long he will sit at the table in the cafeteria, expecting her to burst in like always, terrified.

On the third floor, she gently pushes open the door to Clara's room. In the elevator, she has rehearsed what she will say. But now, as she looks around the door, she sees that Clara is sleeping. Her skin and her hair are pale, crumpled white and she looks bald, close to death.

"It doesn't matter if I make things up to her; she's going to die soon anyway," Jill says to herself.

A sudden impulse makes her want to race back to the cafeteria to catch Cliff before he leaves—beg him to spend the holidays with her as he promised, to repair the months of bad feeling between them.

He'll have left by now, she realizes.

It is almost 5:00. Jill can't bring herself to leave the building. She feels the old, hard need to absorb things driving her, fastening her to the hospital.

Through staircases and back corridors, she makes her way to the orthopedics ward and looks through the window onto the millionaire's estate, but the air is swirling with too much snow to see. In his photographs, the old man is a kind-eyed, smiling person. Jill wonders if he was cruel and moody when he was a young man.

She puts her hand into her pocket and feels something hard. She draws out the key-chain that she has stolen earlier. It is a penny, encased in glass. Turning it over, she reads, "A penny for your thoughts." She remembers the joint that Myra has left with her and decides to go to the basement by herself and smoke it.

The basement of the hospital is a bleakly lit place with many thin corridors and locked rooms—and next to the morgue there is a lounge with overstuffed sofas and a television. The candystripers often come here to smoke a cigarette and talk. As Jill is about to settle herself into one of the sofas to think about things, she notices something—the door of the morgue is ajar. This is Dr. Arnold's domain; once or twice, from the sofa in the lounge, she has spotted him unlocking that door and disappearing into the gloomy depths of that room—a place she can only imagine.

Maybe there's no one in there right now, Jill thinks. I could open the door very carefully and see what a morgue looks like. She debates smoking half of the joint first but slips it into her pocket for later. She doesn't want to waste any time. Someone could come along, see that the door has been accidentally left open, and lock it again. Some opportunities present themselves only once.

The door is heavy and well-oiled. Jill slips inside and instinctively crosses her arms to hug herself. The air is cold and the peculiar smell that she associates with Dr. Arnold permeates the air. There is a row of stainless steel stretchers, each at a slight angle; trolleys with various foreign-looking instruments and white cloths; low-hanging lights.

In the corridor outside, the elevator bell sounds. Jill's heart starts to pound; she will be in serious trouble if she is caught in the morgue. Banging against one of the steel stretchers in her haste, she crouches behind a trolley that is draped with a white sheet. From where she is positioned, she can see Dr. Arnold come in. The unlocked door doesn't appear to concern him.

He is out of sight for a few minutes. Jill is sweating—an unpleasant, sickening sensation in the cold room. The fantasy of meeting Dr. Arnold suddenly terrifies her.

She measures the distance between herself and the door. She hears him rustling with something, a large filing cabinet or drawer being slid open and then a heavy plop, as if a sack of flour had been dropped onto a table.

He is in view again. Through the network of steel legs and cross-bars, she can see that he has brought out a corpse and has arranged the body on one of the stainless steel slabs. The pathologist grunts as he heaves the body over onto its stomach. Jill takes in an involuntary gasp of air. She feels dismayed—horrified at what she has just seen, what she is hearing. There is nothing humane here, nothing gentle and brave. She is glad that his wide back is to her so that she can't see his face.

He'll be cold with Clara, Jill thinks.

She stands up, wincing as her ankles crack. The doctor doesn't hear. Jill glances quickly at the stretcher; the dead person is a man. Not looking back she walks to the door and lets herself out into the corridor. The sound and movement of Dr. Arnold's work behind her stops for a moment. She waits and then walks toward the elevator.

Close Calls

The last August Wendy spent at her uncle's cottage in Haliburton she saw that the poster of Stephanie Baker was gone. She walked through the general store, past the shelves of cottage amusements, and stared at the bulletin board. The square of cork where Stephanie's picture had hung was a deeper brown than the faded corkboard framing it. Everything else on the board looked untouched from the summer before—packages of fishing lures, hooks, lethal-looking sparkling flies, traps, rubber worms.

Wendy glanced around the store; maybe the poster had been moved to another spot. Or a new one put up to replace the old one, which had looked more yellow and torn each year. She went back to the cash register. Her mother was buying things to take to their uncle's cottage: eggs, bread, bacon, orange juice, bags of chips to eat while they played euchre. "You know that girl Stephanie Baker? Her poster's down," Wendy said. She looked at the store owner, ringing up the purchase. She wanted to come right out and accuse him of removing the poster. Of giving up, losing faith. She felt as if someone had stolen, or she herself had lost, something precious. She hadn't expected this. The week in Haliburton and the poster of Stephanie Baker's disappearance went together. She felt cheated, as if time were moving along too

144

fast. She hadn't been given a chance.

She had been daydreaming about Stephanie Baker for years. By the poster's description, Wendy knew they were the same age, but Stephanie had long straight blond hair and a sweet, even-tempered, smiling face. She had not been frozen at ten years old. She had grown into her teens with Wendy, a perfect friend that Wendy met and rescued from Northern Ontario lake-pirates or kidnappers looking for ransom. A favourite fantasy involved white-slave traders. Stephanie had been stolen for her blond beauty, her virginity. She was drugged and being kept—where? Sometimes in a winterized, but isolated cottage; sometimes in a cave or in the back of a van. She was always unharmed whenever Wendy found her—except in one or two daydreams which got stretched too far and Stephanie's spirit was deadened by the time Wendy arrived. Her wish to live had dried up. Her beautiful hair and face were grey and withered like an old woman's. She might have been beaten or tortured. The horror of these things was not imaginable in a real way.

In every dream, Wendy risked her life to save Stephanie. Once, she even died rescuing Stephanie.

"Did they find that girl?" Mrs. Seldon asked, lifting her eyebrows doubtfully at the store owner.

He shook his head, which was over-sized and nearly bald, tufted by grey hair at the crown of his head. He punched the keys on the cash register. "Only leave a reward notice up for five years or so." He did not look at them. When Wendy's father came into the store each summer, this man had a joke to share, always a smile. Even with Bill, two years younger than Wendy, he'd have a few words and a wink. Women didn't quite measure up. Each summer, he pretended never to have seen Wendy or her mother before.

Wendy stared at the man and realized that he would, from here on in, figure in her daydreams as a culprit.

"She might still show up," Wendy said to her mother weakly.

"Whatever you do, don't be as stupid as that poor foolish little girl," Mrs. Seldon said as she reached out a ten-dollar bill.

Wendy tried to carry the memory of Stephanie Baker's photograph in front of her eyes, but after a few months it began to fade. She felt that she was betraying a trustworthy, constant friend, a central figure in her girlhood dreams. But she wasn't dreaming that kind of dream much anymore. She couldn't look directly at Stephanie in her mind now.

By Christmas, Wendy's hair, which she had been growing out for a long time, was to her waist. She ironed it to make it gleam and hang even straighter. Her brother's was shoulder-length. The fights between him and their parents were becoming fierce. Wendy and her girlfriend Sue-Ellen wore short skirts, eye shadow by Yardley, and earrings shaped like hearts from Kresges. Each night before turning the light out, Wendy sat in her bedroom and raised the hems on her dresses and skirts. Every afternoon, when she returned home from highschool, her mother had let the hems back down. Not a word was ever said.

She had started to go out on dates—and with older guys. It disappointed her to discover that they were not as smart, not as smooth or relaxed as she had expected. She met John, a law student in his early twenties, who drove a red convertible sports car. His parents were well-to-do and owned a large grocery store in town so the Seldons allowed Wendy to go out with him, despite the fact he was eight years older. He was in law school at Osgoode Hall, which impressed Wendy's parents.

One night near Christmas he drove Wendy up to Toronto to the house of another law student. It might

146

have been where he stayed while going to classes. There was a Christmas tree decorated with lights and icicles in the living room.

"I'll leave you two alone," the other guy said. He winked at John. She felt sorry that he was leaving the room since he was handsome, moreso than John, and in a way that resembled the man she had begun to fantasize marrying some day. But she felt he was a bit silly—he had underestimated her by winking like that.

John pretended to conduct an interview with her. They sat on the floor by the Christmas tree, drinking and smoking a joint. He leaned forward, holding an imaginary microphone, and asked her questions.

"And what do you think of sex?" he asked finally into his fisted hand before stretching it across to Wendy's mouth.

She had been stumped by that. The answer— that she was a virgin and terrified—wasn't something she had the nerve to reveal. What she knew was that the act he was putting on made him transparent. She felt above him suddenly, furious that he and the winking law-school friend dismissed her as small and unimportant. When he loomed over her and pressed her backward onto the shag carpet, pulling at her clothes and burying his face in her neck, she felt only the slightest fear. Although she was quite drunk and stoned, and his weight on her was suffocating, two facts remained clear in her head: he was in law school and there was another man in the house to hear her if she screamed. She announced it was time he took her home.

She had an image of herself as a whirling solitary figure, moving through dazzling events. She liked the belief that no one knew the real Wendy—and that she had dipped only a toe into the vastness of her life.

One night, when she came in from being downtown at the Globe restaurant with Sue-Ellen, eating shoestrings and gravy and drinking coke, Wendy found a letter from her mother lying on her pillow. The blankets and sheets had been pulled back as if the bed had been prepared for a hotel guest.

In the letter, Mrs. Seldon said she had always loved Wendy and that she had always wanted a baby girl and how thrilled she had been when Wendy was born. She wondered what had gone wrong. Wendy could hear her mother's careful, deliberate, ferocious tone in the letter. It ended with an announcement: No socializing on weeknights, and a curfew of midnight on Fridays and Saturdays.

"But I have to go out on weeknights," she said to her mother the next morning at the breakfast table. "Everyone else goes out. Anyway, I'm the one who gets the high marks."

"If you stayed home, your marks would be even higher," her father said.

"Look at what happened to that girl in the poster, what was her name—" her mother began.

"Stephanie."

"Look at what happened to her."

But Wendy, who had carried Stephanie around like a favourite character in a book—perhaps Mary in *The Secret Garden* or one of the pony-riding girls in an English novel—could not see what had happened. There was nowhere to look. When she looked at all, she saw beautiful Stephanie Baker with her blond hair fanned out over a lot of deep rich grass in spring, her eyes closed as if asleep. Or her hair rising underwater like the petals of a sunflower, her eyes closed and her lips open, iridescent bubbles rising past sunken treasure to the surface.

Mrs. Seldon shook her head and set her mouth as if she were gritting her teeth to clamp down on a wave of nausea. She shook her head and looked away from Wendy at the kitchen wall. "Don't you ever. . . ." She stopped short.

It was unusual, because generally Wendy could

148

rely on her mother to provide a graphic portrait of any person's tragedy. When Wendy had first tried water-skiing at the Haliburton cottage and had not known to let go of the line as she neared the dock, Mrs. Seldon had been walking to the shore with her Instamatic. She happened to snap a picture just as Wendy was about to be sliced in half by the jutting diving board. The photograph turned out to be a blur of Wendy contorting sideways at the last minute, a red smear of blood where the diving board grazed her waist as she flew past.

Afterwards Mrs. Seldon relished showing the photograph to people, and shivering and rolling her eyes. She always related a story to go with the photograph—of a boy who had water-skied at a high speed into a face of granite cliff bordering a lake. When he arrived dead at a nearby hospital, nothing but pulp and blood, the emergency nurse was his own sister.

In January, there was an ad in the paper for part-time sales clerks at Simpsons. Wendy applied and got a position in the young women's clothing department. In the mall, she met Gary, who worked as a sales clerk in a men's wear store. He was even older than John. Wendy felt that it was best to lie about his age to her parents. One night, he drove her to Toronto. They went to Yorkville first and walked up and down the streets looking at the hippies. They bought two marijuana cigarettes and drove out to the airport and smoked them in the car. They went inside the terminal to buy chips and pop and sat eating in silence, paralyzed by the drugs and the screaming chaos of a group of Italians who had just gotten off a plane. He told Wendy, in a sad, old-man's voice, about his first love--a girl he had finally given up on when she told him at the top of a ski hill in Collingwood, "I've still got you wrapped around my little finger." The next day, Wendy couldn't remember driving home from the airport.

"You mean he doesn't go to school! I thought you

knew him from school," Mrs. Seldon said after pressing for information one night at dinner and discovering that he worked full-time in the men's wear store.

"How old is this fellow?" Wendy's father said, his face compressing and creasing as if she had just announced she was fatally ill.

Revised guidelines were imposed: Wendy was to date boys, not men. Nineteen was the cut-off age.

Wendy's parents had not gone to school long, and they wanted their children to do well. They were self-taught. Each weekend they lugged home books from the library in order to keep abreast of changes. All anyone talked about was the rate at which the world was expanding. Every morning, Wendy and her family listened to the radio's litany of murder, political dishonour, and human cruelty. Most of the events were staged in small, unheard-of towns in the States that became landmarks overnight, because of mass murders or appalling tornadoes—something Wendy thought she would like to experience just as Dorothy had in Kansas with Toto. She'd like to see that twister crossing the Kansas farm fields—a black, soul-shaking funnel of dust and terror.

Mrs. Seldon often sighed after putting down a newspaper. "It'll be the last straw when we have to lock our doors before going to bed at night."

Things were happening in broad daylight—assassinations, muggings, armed bank hold-ups. It seemed impossible for journalists to get clear photographs of the people who committed the most horrible crimes—as if the criminals were missing some parts. Their pictures in the paper and on television were blurred and indistinct like the ones of Lee Harvey Oswald, Albert de Salvo. As if there were less than a full human life for the camera to capture.

In February, everyone was amused when one of the neighbours—a woman notorious for looking through her curtains and observing everyone's activities during the day—peered out her window in the middle of the night and saw a dark figure stalking through an adjoining yard. The woman called the police, who were quickly on the scene, shining their flashlights into the snow-covered backyards, finally revealing the culprit—a snowman that some children had made during the day.

"Never you mind," Mrs. Seldon said after she had told Wendy and Bill the story and they sat around the dinner table snickering at the neighbour's foolishness. "Doesn't it make you feel good to know she had the gumption to call the police?"

Mr. Seldon agreed. "In this case she was wrong, but what if it had been a prowler? We're lucky to have good neighbours."

Bill scoffed. "Who's going to prowl in February?"

The conversation switched to a girl at school who had gotten pregnant. At one time, she had come to the house to take piano lessons from Mrs. Seldon.

"Poor, foolish girl," Mr. Seldon said soberly, shaking his head and staring at his coffee cup.

This comment was directed at Wendy. She knew it and so did her brother. She glanced at him and caught the smug expression on his face.

"I've got to get going," Wendy said, looking at the clock on the wall. "The meeting starts at seven."

"I'll drive you," Mr. Seldon announced.

"I can take the bus."

After Christmas—and after getting the letter from her mother that restricted the number of nights she could be out—Wendy had joined The Leo Club. It was the junior chapter of the Lions Club and a man who was a manager at Simpsons had encouraged Wendy and the other young girls at the store to join. She was appointed secretary. A girl Wendy's age with an advanced, sophisticated manner was appointed president.

"Why won't you let me drive you?" Mr. Seldon

said.

Wendy shrugged. She pulled on her mittens and wrapped along purple scarf around her neck. "Maybe I'll call you to come and get me."

Her father looked offended.

It was a sharp winter night. At a dip in the road, the woods and the houses of a more distant neighbourhood were silhouetted against the twilight sky. It was only six and already the street was quiet. It was the season when people made excuses to stay in.

Shifting from one foot to the other, Wendy played with the snow about the bus stop, scooping it into a small mound and running her boot heel down the sides so that the melting snow would re-freeze into ice. Balancing on the slippery, gleaming sides, she could look down and make out the layers of water freezing as each surface turned to ice. Across the street, the light from a kitchen lit up the snow of a back yard and its now famous lopsided snowman, a dark scarf draped about its peculiar, neckless torso. A hockey rink in the next yard was strung with yellow lights.

The cold passed through Wendy's ski jacket and chilled her unbearably. She pressed her mittens to her face and felt her pinched white skin. She tightened the scarf about her neck and hugged her coat to her body, hands thrust into her pockets. She was tempted to walk home, give up the idea of going to the Leo Club meeting. But they were going to the Globe restaurant afterwards for shoestrings and gravy. At home, her father's pipe smoke and the roar of the hockey game would filter through the walls to Wendy's bedroom. And her parents would seize the opportunity to continue their harangue about homework, Wendy's choice of friends, the length of her skirts.

The cold was freezing the air that she breathed and making her gulp. In the winter, the bus was often late, held up by traffic toward the town line where the network of factories began or by a snowplow, or a block in the road. Sometimes, the driver stopped at the city limits for a coffee in the bowling alley behind the gas station—and a ten-minute talk with the fat, made-up waitress who served donuts and coffee in styrofoam cups. The bowling alley was a seedy place with coke-and-hamburger ads thumbtacked against a dull green wall. Sometimes, fights broke out in the parking lot.

"I don't want to hear that you've been hanging around that place," Mrs. Seldon told Wendy more than once, darkly. "It'll be all anyone can talk about. Once people decide something, it's hard to change their minds."

Wendy and Bill were somehow diplomatic representatives to the world, the guardians of their parents' reputation.

Each time the bowling-alley conversation ensued, Wendy turned her face away so that her mother wouldn't guess she had already, out of curiosity, ventured into the place. Her daydreams about Stephanie Baker had given her a sense of what it was to disappear and be a poster on a fading bulletin board. She wanted to make her life chock-full of things-happened, just in case. She wanted to have more experiences than she could remember. It would be no good to disappear like Stephanie—be imprisoned somewhere and have a lot of wide open space in her heart and head where memory and sensation could have vibrated instead.

She continued to massage the pyramid of ice, feeling in the darkness that each side was as smooth as the next. Over the roofs of the houses, Orion was clearly a Greek god ready to hunt. The beam of headlights illuminated the sky over the crest of the hill and headed toward her.

Just in time, Wendy thought. She had been on the verge of turning back. She fumbled in her pocket for the fare and groaned as she realized that the lights weren't those of the bus.

A station wagon slowed down for the corner, its tires slipping on patches of snow missed by the grader. The driver looked in both directions and began to pull away. Then, he hesitated and glanced out of the car at Wendy. He waved as if he recognized her. Leaning forward, she peered through the darkness. A muffled tune from the radio trembled against the windows of the car, which was jerking as if the motor were about to stall.

It was too dark to see. The door swung open and the heat of the car's interior flowed into the night air. The driver withdrew his hand. "Heading downtown. Want a lift?"

Wendy pictured the bus driver with his hand in his pocket, leaning comfortably on the counter, the waitress with sugar donuts on tea-cup saucers, resting her elbows on the counter near him.

He'll notice that I'm hesitating, Wendy realized. She felt embarrassed. If she had to wait much longer for the bus, she would be late for the meeting. "That would be great!"

"Hop in then."

She slid onto the seat and leaned back awkwardly when the driver reached in front of her to pull the door shut. They started away and Wendy turned and smiled at him. She wondered whether she should tell him something about herself—what school she attended or why she was going downtown. He was bound to think she was ungrateful or rude if she sat without talking. She thought these things drowsily. The warm air rushing from the vents was affecting her like warm milk or flannelette sheets.

"Thank you for stopping," she said. Her teeth clicked like hard sharp pieces of marble. "I'm going downtown to a Leo Club meeting." This fact tended to impress adults. Maybe she went to school with one of this man's kids.

"Fine." He nodded and continued to drive in

silence.

She had never come across anyone who didn't ask what the Leo Club was.

He's not interested in talking, she thought. Relieved to be out of the winter night and on her way, she settled back and let the familiarity of passing homes mark the route. In the gully between the church and Conlin's store she saw some girls from school—Sue-Ellen among them—with skates across their shoulders. She waved and then realized they wouldn't recognize the car.

"Friends of mine," Wendy said.

She tried to look over her shoulder at her girl-friends but the window was fogged over. Sue-Ellen was having the same problems at home that Wendy was having. The two of them left school each day at lunch with Tom, a boy in their class who had his own car, a silver-grey Camaro. They drove to Dines restaurant at the mall and ordered hamburgers, onion rings, and milkshakes. They always smoked a joint on the way over and ended up stuffing the food into their mouths like wadding.

Wendy had been in trouble over this. She had been selected to act as a prefect in the cafeteria at lunch during certain days of the week. The vice-principal had made a production of giving her a school sweater with the school's colours—gold, brown and white—on the arms. But it had been reported that she kept missing her prefect duty, and he had called her in.

She had never been called into a principal's office before. This man had a savage reputation.

"What's the matter with you?" he asked her.

He was a man with a permanently exasperated face. He asked her this in a fatherly way and she felt taken aback. She had expected him to be harsh. Her eyes filled with tears because she thought maybe he was right and something was wrong with her. She shook her head

155

and shrugged her shoulders, trembling. Suddenly, she recognized his strategy. He was manipulating her, figuring out the best way, the quickest and cleanest, to get at her.

She had handed in her prefect sweater and only felt badly once or twice when she and Sue-Ellen went to Dine's in Tom's Camaro.

She took her mittens off and resisted the urge to rub the window clear of fog. People didn't like that because it streaked the glass. Wendy had not gotten over her childhood enjoyment of writing her initials with great style and flourish on steamy windows. The radio was playing country and western music but it was distorted by interference, too much treble. The lights of downtown began to brighten the sky ahead and Wendy thought lethargically how reluctant she was to have to step outside again.

Snapping out of a daze, she saw they had taken a turn onto a street which headed north for some ways and eventually led out of town. She looked around to orient herself: a different neighbourhood, but a familiar one. Her grandmother lived three blocks from here.

The driver's expression had not changed. With one hand on the wheel, he continued at the same speed. It seemed more polite not to point out that this was an unusual route to town. He could be taking a different way. Who am I to know all the roads? Wendy thought. But she felt uncertain. He had created a barrier, an odd feeling in the car, by refusing to speak.

The houses were getting shabbier as they neared the edge of town. Driveways were cluttered with snowy bed springs, old motors, broken chairs, tires, and cords of wood. Wendy recognized a house where she had attended a birthday party years earlier—a girl from her Grade three class, from a poor, ill-fated family, who nevertheless had had a wonderful birthday party. The mother had led a noisy, foot-kicking bunny hop around

156

the living room.

They continued northwards in tight, constrained silence. Wider spaces between houses. No one was walking along the road.

Wendy realized she had to speak. She tried to think of something courteous to say. She forced the words past her lips. "Are you going downtown?"

"I'm going up ahead a ways," the man said, lifting his hand from the steering wheel to gesture.

She stared at his hand which was enormous, a fleshy baseball mitt.

"I have to pick up a friend who works with me on the night shift," he added, without looking at Wendy.

He was forty, she thought, maybe fifty. When he had pulled up at the bus stop, she had assumed he was somebody's father, a neighbour, someone whose house she had visited on Halloween nights. Not many people drove down her street at six o'clock unless they lived in the neighbourhood.

As the landscape slipped by, Wendy pretended to be watching it. What he had said could easily be true. The factories in town did have night shifts. She looked sideways and saw that his lips were pursed to whistle but nothing was coming out. With a jolt, she knew that something was wrong. She looked ahead again and began to pull at bits of fluff—tiny balls of wool on the mittens that her mother had knit. Wendy cleared her throat.

"Where is it that you work?"

The Leo Club meeting would already be started. She could walk in late—but what if one of them was trying to call her at home right now? "Mrs. Seldon, we're wondering why Wendy is late." Her parents would be helpless, beside themselves.

A knot tightened in her stomach.

The stranger named a factory in the city which produced sheet metal. His voice rose naturally.

He'll turn around and go back before long, Wendy assured herself. But where will the other man sit?

The prospect of a second silent and menacing stranger in the car made her dizzy.

From the corner of her eye, Wendy looked at the driver. Above the fur collar of his dark green parka rose his featureless face, double-chinned and shadowy. Wendy's face twitched. Her left eye fluttered for the first time in years. She touched it with her finger. A feeling of panic, painful and trembling, gripped her heart. She tried to calm herself: Tell him to stop if he isn't going to drive straight downtown, she rehearsed. Tell him to let me out, thank you, and I can walk from here.

The words kept dying in her mouth.

Trusting, waiting things out, felt safer, easier. He would turn back. Or he would meet his friend and then drive back to town.

They passed another patch of houses. The scratchy radio music was being drowned out as the road became rougher, making the paint-spattered ladders and tools clang in the rear. Wendy turned in her seat to look at them and, lifting her eyes, saw through the back window that the city's lights were disappearing into the distance. She faced ahead again.

"Where does this friend of yours live? I don't want to be late and I probably already am." Wendy bit her lip. Was that too anxious? Too rude? She didn't want him to know how frightened she was. Somehow, her safety lay in concealing that.

"He lives close to here."

She waited as they rushed into the darkness. Every mile or so, a farmhouse appeared, set back in a field, aglow with lights. Wendy was struck by an image of her parents relaxing in the overly warm living room at home, reading, watching TV. Her father would still be feeling annoyed that she had insisted on going out on a weeknight, even if it was for a Leo Club meeting.

Through a farmhouse window, Wendy saw people moving through their evening rituals, unaware of what was racing past them. A sensation passed through her chest—she had been lifted outside of normal life; she was on the other side of a screen, apart from what was safe, knowable.

She sat stiffly on the seat, waiting for this strange, unbelievable moment to end. After another space of silence had passed, she said loudly, "Where are you going?" She felt her heart racing, partly from the belief that she was insulting this man, a good Samaritan who had stopped to give her a lift on a freezing winter night. This had to be awkward for him. She had the odd feeling that it might be her job to protect him from feeling awkward—or from picking up on her own tension.

She stared hard at the driver's face, then at the road, and back again at his face, trying to will him to look at her, to stop the car from heading into the depths of the countryside, taking her with it. The night was suddenly a place she hadn't known existed.

This time, the man remained silent.

She decided to throw herself from the car as soon as he began to slow down.

Even if he doesn't slow down, she thought, I'll throw myself out. It would be better to land in a ditch of snow—better even to be hurt in the fall. In a quick succession of blurred images, she imagined being run over by the car, dying from exposure once she began to search her way back to town, being pursued in a field, tackled.

She reached down in the darkness of the station wagon to touch the handle. A sick feeling vibrated through her body. She stared down through the green pallor cast by the dashboard and saw that the handles had been broken off the knobs.

She put her mittens back on, took them off, plucked at the wool. Her heart bolted inside her chest.

He would turn to face her. What would he say? What would she do? This can't be happening, she said to herself. This can't happen. Her life was something that was too real for this to happen. What did he want? She had never had to fight with a man. He'll rape me, Wendy thought. She could not visualize it further than that: just the word itself dangling in the blackness inside her head. But rape was often followed by murder. He wouldn't want her to be able to identify him. ... None of this would happen. None of it could happen. Not to me, Wendy thought.

They were now miles from the neighbourhood where she had waited for the bus. She thought suddenly of Stephanie Baker. The pressure and chill of nausea swelled in her throat. Maybe the girl had just run away. But not for six years. She might have gone through the thoughts Wendy was thinking now. Maybe she had been knocked unconscious first and then killed. Wendy had never considered her own death before. Not as something this close. Death was an old woman in a narrow bed, gaunt and leather-faced, hands folded, yellow lace, ready to pass on.

She looked out the car window. There were no street lights now, no fences. It was scarcely a road that they were on. She had no idea where they were. She knew only that they were heading north, away from town. The stars were behind them.

The car came slowly to a stop and the engine shuddered. A fallen fence lay across the path—or maybe he had driven down a dead-end country lane. He turned on the seat to face her.

Unable to stop herself, she said, "What?"

He stared, unblinking, at her. "Is it worth a kiss to get back home?"

Wendy stared back at him. "No, I can't." Her voice no longer belonged to her. "No!" she cried as he moved his hand along the back of the seat toward her head.

He leaned against his door. "Isn't it worth a kiss to get back?"

Somewhere, Wendy heard the sound of doubt. He was unsure. He had never done something like this before. She would do it. She would lean across the seat and kiss him—quickly, the completion of an agreement, an arrangement. She would kiss him and then back away and he would keep the promise he had made. But what if he didn't. The voices in her body were drowning each other out, but the deepest one, the judging one, was a bass humming noise, the strongest voice there, something close and essential speaking to her, calling.

If I kiss him, I'm dead, Wendy heard herself thinking.

He would take the kiss as a sign of weakness, of encouragement. She remained frozen, the round door knobs pressing into her jacket. She let the voice deep in her throat that was desperate and shrewd have its way— she began to plead with him. She twisted the mittens in her hands.

"Take me home—I promise I'll never tell anyone a word of this. I'll never describe you. Just take me home."

She explored his face with her eyes and pleaded.

In the darkness of the car, his face changed expression. He smirked. "How old are you?"

"Sixteen." Should have said fourteen, thirteen, the voice in the back of her head said.

"You're awfully foolish to have taken a ride with me."

"Yes," Wendy said, barely audible. She felt a quick fury at his fatherly, reprimanding tone of voice.

His arm shot out. Wendy screamed and realized that he had tried to scare her back into muteness, passivity.

"Let me go, I'll find my own way home. Leave me here," she begged him. Maybe she was going to be all right. He wasn't going to carry out some dimly formed plan in his head after all.

"Get out of here, then," he said. He reached in front of her and she shrank against the car seat. He grasped the knob and wrenched it around.

The car door flew open, and the winter night cut its way into the car. As he leaned forward and grabbed her purple scarf, Wendy rolled past the open door onto the snow. She felt the scarf tightening around her neck. Twisting, she released a faint scream and whirled dizzily so that the scarf unwrapped and the stranger was left tightening it in his grip.

In great awkward leaps, she floundered through snow drifts. A fence post rose ahead of her, a foot above the snow. She pinned her eyes to the wood that someone's safe, methodical hand had lowered into the ground.

He's after me, Wendy thought wildly. He would catch her. She tasted something strong in her mouth. Any minute, he would bury her in the snow beneath his weight. She listened past her heaving breath to catch him behind her and, in mid-motion, shot a look back. The tail lights of the car were moving up the laneway, already a half-mile into the deep darkness of the countryside.

She kept fighting her way through the snow, falling and gasping from the exertion. She scanned the eerie blue-black night. She would call Tom. She would give directions. He would drive to get her in his Camaro. He would drive her home and she would never tell her parents what had happened.

A light flashed in the distance and Wendy saw a farm's yellow windows through a stand of trees. She stopped to rest her heart and catch her breath and wonder at still being alive. She felt the sudden, strange triumph of having escaped something inescapable—of knowing what others had known, but never lived to tell. She thought of Stephanie's poster and tried to see beyond it to a vast twisted darkness until the image evaporated in her mind.

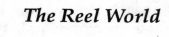

The Reel World

Meeting him had been innocent enough. A new two-storey Simpsons had opened and when a contest was held to select one girl from each of the high schools in town to represent her schoolmates in the Fashion and Cosmetic sections of the store, Aileen Mason was chosen from hers. It was a great coup to be the one selected since everyone in town was excited about having Simpsons to shop at and many girls had vied for the position. And when the afternoon arrived to sit for the glossy black-and-white promotional portraits, Ralph Brown was asked to do the photography. åIf Simpsons had hired him, then he had to be good, people thought, or at least professional enough, just as if it had been Eatons who hired him, or any of the stores in Canada which represented everything familiar right across the country. It established the man's reputation.

The girls were asked to wait in one of the store lounges. They sat shyly, smiling, regarding each other's dresses and shoes, while one by one each of them was led by the Advertising Manager into the committee room. The man waiting with his camera was Ralph—a short but gangling man, fortyish, with something birdlike about his face which was pale, almost smooth as a boy's hairless chin; his eyes seemed lidless like a chicken's.

Aileen was nervous but proud. That morning, she had washed her hair and conditioned it with eggs; she had made herself up with meticulous care. The portraits were destined to be enlarged and put not only on display in the store's front window for two weeks, but also in the town newspaper. Thousands would see them. But just as Aileen was settling down onto the chair that Ralph had provided, she felt uncomfortable and almost helpless, knowing that so much depended on how well her picture turned out. Her face felt chalky suddenly, ladened down by its powder and blue-grey mascara.

Later, Aileen was too embarrassed to ask the other girls what Ralph had been like with them. In her case, he was flattering but not insincerely, she decided. He surprised her by asking whether she had modelled before, she had a good face, fine structure; why even her hands themselves would be perfect for modelling. The sense of wearing some sort of flimsy mask, of not being well put together, lessened; she found herself smiling almost naturally.

"Maybe you'd be interested in picking up a few dollars doing some modelling work for me on weekends," Ralph said. "When you're not working here," he added.

The prospect of her own face, its particular expressions being captured and later admired by strangers, perhaps by relatives, friends, excited Aileen. Everyone in town would shop at Simpsons and see her picture— this one and any that Ralph might take in the future. She traced an outline in her mind, imagining old ladies with pillbox hats and heavy melton-wool coats, and guys, boys from school, all leaning over to look more closely at her picture in the store window, in the newspaper, on walls in buildings she herself had never been in.

"Can't pay you much, maybe with pictures," Ralph told her. "Just getting started myself."

She gave him her phone number, and when she got home that afternoon and explained the invitation to her parents, they were impressed. He was a married man after all, a professional; Aileen had learned that his wife, named Brenda, worked in an office but was on leave to have their first baby.

* * *

A cool wind was blowing off Lake Erie and across the park on Saturday afternoon. There was a lot of gear to carry. Ralph locked the car and he and Aileen began to walk briskly—because Aileen was only wearing a thigh-length tee-shirt that Ralph had supplied, which read "Midas Muffler"—across the field and past a few pic-nickers at the table and bench area. As the strangers paused in their loud, boisterous talk to observe Aileen and Ralph, she felt appalled at what they must have been seeing. She felt silly in her costume on a cold day like this. Ralph wouldn't have noticed her sudden silence; she had been at a loss for anything to say since he picked her up. This was her first "session" with him. She didn't know exactly what to call him—Mr. Brown sounded childish. So she avoided having to use his name at all, afraid of disappointing him with her schoolgirl demeanour. He, on the other hand, was relaxed and had done most of the talking on the way over in the car.

When they had passed and were at the edge of the clearing, Ralph shifted his tripod and lens case to one arm and took something out of his right pocket. Aileen, looking sideways, saw that he had brought a joint along which surprised her because Ralph couldn't have been much younger than her own father. But then, he was an artist—they did things like this.

"Ever tried pot?" Ralph said, darting his tongue along either side of the paper. He talked like that—never in complete sentences as if it were a waste of time. His speech was punctuated by grammatical slips; said seen instead of saw, but he wasn't what you would have called stupid.

166

"Of course I have," Aileen said quickly, with just a hint of self-righteousness.

Ralph lit it and with a touch of camaraderie, the new kind that went along with doing something underground—acceptable but illicit—handed the acrid-smelling joint to Aileen. They laughed at the noises their inhaling breaths made. She regretted, then, having been afraid to call him by his name. Once they were in the woods, she stood amid a group of treetrunks and parted the lower branches; her eyes gleamed through the leaves to meet Ralph's camera. She felt herself looking beautiful, professional.

She was aware that something was happening. The camera and the photographer behind it were injecting her, across the empty space, with enormous new strength. She had never felt anything like it. This peculiar new feeling—a kind of heightened, dizzy self-awareness—must be felt by photographer's models all over the world, the famous ones, Aileen thought . . . the exhilaration of the reeling camera. Her earlier qualms at being seen by the people lunching in the park disappeared. She found herself wishing she had been prouder, graceful, aloof—the way you expected a model to look.

When they returned to the car, Ralph discovered he had locked his keys inside. Aileen was tired; they had taken pictures for more than an hour, and the sight of purplish-coloured goosebumps rising on her legs and the breeze off the lake running the hair on her arms backwards, made her irritable but she stood to the side, arms crossed quietly in case anyone should be watching. That Ralph would do something as foolish, as unprofessional, as lock his keys in bothered her. There they were, dangling from the ignition through the glass, a rubber mermaid hanging motionless from one of the chains. A member of the picnickers, an absurdly-shaped man who couldn't speak English, wearing nothing but a pair of baggy white underwear, wandered over with a clothes-hanger which he had somehow retrieved and helped get the car door open. The sight of the fat old man and Ralph bending seriously over the windowpane amused Aileen and she decided that, rather than be annoyed, she would chalk the afternoon up to three hours of adventure.

The pictures didn't turn out well.

Some could have been called sexy but her stomach protruded in the lateral shots and in all of them, her eyes were slanted and stoned-looking.

Ralph had arranged a dropping-off place where Aileen could pick the composite sheets up without having to undergo the embarrassment of being asked to share the pictures with anyone else, and they were stored in her locker at school. Not that there was anything to object to, although the Midas Muffler tee-shirt was zealously tight and in one shot, which Ralph had taken candidly of Aileen sitting on a fence rail, her knees weren't posed; between her legs she could make out the dark triangle of her underwear. Her head was averted because she had been in the act of shifting to get a secure seat. Ralph laughed it off: "Not a model alive doesn't pose nude eventually—part of the game, gotta do it; want to get ahead?"

"When are we going to see some of those pictures of you?" Mr. Mason said one night at dinner. He had a spare rib in his mouth; his eyes stayed on the meat as he spoke.

"So far, he hasn't made me copies," Aileen said, faltering.

"Never heard of a model getting paid with her own pictures, but then this is a small town," Mr. Mason said.

Aileen thought quickly. "I'll bring some home for you to see. Some of them are quite good; Ralph promised to blow them up for us." She added "us" at the last minute—a clever move, she thought safely to herself.

She didn't have to fight with her father, whose allegiance she valued. It was her mother who was always at her. The world she tried to impose on Aileen seemed impossibly distant, a nebulous place anymore but one which Aileen understood she might easily have resigned herself to years ago had she been weaker. It was hard to take seriously, especially now that she was working part-time at Simpsons and studying with Ralph to be a model. Sometimes when she was standing folding sweaters at a counter in the store, she'd catch herself suddenly in one of the three-way mirrors about the Department and be pleasantly taken aback at how fine she looked. If only Ralph could be here now, she'd think. She liked to imagine him following her with the lens, kneeling behind a shelf across the store, focusing the telescopic eye, preserving a moment of flushing beauty in her face.

It was raining the next weekend. They had originally planned to go to the lake and get some bathing suit shots.

"Portfolio needs a full-length swimsuit shot," Ralph had said confidently.

The portfolio was comprised so far by a large facial shot which Aileen was mildly disappointed by because she had been tired that morning and her face looked puffy; the large red beginnings of a pimple drew one's eye to her forehead. It irritated her that she couldn't rely on Ralph for better judgment. In other ways he was incredibly attentive; he had taken her career as a model into his own hands. Next, a shot of Aileen in a yellow chiffon evening gown, the only colour shot, which she also secretly disliked because of the gown's shapelessness which made her look like a double-yellow popsicle. And three shots of different outfits, different poses.

"We'll take some in the studio," Ralph said over the phone on the rainy morning. "Bring three, four outfits."

"Where's his studio?" Mrs. Mason asked, coming into the kitchen on the transparent pretence of adding sugar to her morning coffee.

"At his place by the shopping centre," Aileen said,

not looking at her mother whose face tightened, but out the window instead as she began to think of the dresses she would need.

"Will his wife be there?" her mother continued.

"Of course," Aileen said accusingly.

In her bedroom, she selected three dresses from the closet and began to put a fourth one on. Through her bedroom window, she looked out upon the backyard, richly soaked by the sodden grey clouds, so low and impenetrable that sunshine for another day at least was unlikely. Looking out at the cold colourless day suddenly tranquillized her. She thought of the afternoon ahead with Ralph and felt herself uncontrollably slowing down, the blood in her veins thickening to the consistency of molasses. She woodenly raised her arms and let a yellow rayon dress fall over the shoulders.

"My brain's like porridge," she giggled.

She brushed her hair and sat on the edge of the bed to do so. It had grown almost to her waist, shiny as a Philippine's and healthy as vinegar. She tilted her head, letting the hair fall further down her back. An interesting pose. One to use with Ralph some time. In the mirror, she pulled the dress flat about her body till every curve of flesh was pressed tight.

* * *

"Why not try this?"

Aileen followed Ralph's voice down the hallway and into his and his wife's bedroom. The bed was made but the dresser top was cluttered by empty glasses, and ashtrays, books on photography, and a few Playboy magazines. She picked one up and leafed through it quickly, then put it down again.

Ralph held up a lacy, expensive-looking, sheer nightgown. His wife was having a few problems and was in the hospital.

170

"Whose is it?" Aileen asked casually, unnecessarily. "Brenda's?" She reached forward as if to examine the cloth more closely, to give herself time. If I say no, he'll be angry, maybe want to stop working with me, think I'm afraid.

The thrill of the pictures—reel after reel being consumed by her face, her body, her clothes—and then the day she received the manila envelope bulging with pictures, were the most exciting things she had ever experienced, a virtual adventure. Everything these days—the pictures, the attention and the reaction of her two best girlfriends at her incredibly good luck—it was all too important to risk.

She looked at herself differently now, regarded herself with a professional set of eyes, hundreds of eyes from inside and outside, which watched and constantly gauged her. It was not like conceit; she was not putting on airs—she watched herself scrupulously to make sure of it.

"OK, but nothing too revealing," she said, turning in into a joke with her grin. She took the nightgown from Ralph's outstretched hand and waited till he left the room.

There are girls who would put this on, get into bed and call him in, Aileen thought as she stood before the mirror. It was how you got ahead. The dark circle of her nipples was visible through the cloth; in fact, the gauzy quality of the fabric worked like a magnifying glass and her nipples looked bigger than was true. She pulled the negligee tight across her hipbones and looked at herself again in the mirror before going out to the living room.

Photography wasn't Ralph's only mainline. Now that Brenda was pregnant—a large, glassy, unlikely-looking woman, according to a portrait on the bookcase—and for the sake of this condominium, he was holding down two jobs; he worked in a factory somewhere south of town most days. He had one other girl coming to model besides Aileen.

"But when is anything going to start happening to me?" Aileen asked him as she walked onto the white silky roll of backdrop paper. The lights blinded her momentarily. She felt her nipples harden. "Have you heard whether the tee-shirt shot was bought up?"

Ralph hadn't looked up yet. He was busy adjusting wires and screws and inserting the rectangular reels of film into the Hassleblad. "Midas bought the one from the morning in the park. Going *Sports Illustrated* early spring. Good news 'bout something else, too," he said and he looked up then, grinning so that the space where his tooth was missing gaped darkly and his ears which were always thin and pointed seemed to straighten even more, stretch upwards. He brushed his hand over his almost hairless scalp. It was fairly long where it was still growing at the back.

"What!"

"Live modelling, mannequin work, runway modelling."

"Where? When!"

"Mid-Village Mall—not sure when; let you know by next weekend," he promised. "Up on this."

He carried a black vinyl bar stool across and set it on the crinkling white paper. The promise of live modelling had set her off. She put her heart into the pictures and imagined them someday being published on expensive, satin paper: people examining the early days of her career preserved by the camera.

They were seductive shots. Aileen studied them carefully a few days later. In her favourite, she had her feet stretched out behind and both palms leaning hard and forward on the stool, with Ralph snapping her from a distance above, standing on a small stepladder; she had looked up through her lashes at him and barely smiled. Her breasts showed tight and round through the nightgown .

* * *

Unlike most of their sessions, she was at Ralph's home on a weeknight since he was busy on the weekend. His second model had an interview at Eatons Catalogue Office. Aileen felt hurt and disappointed. For a week, she had been studying the magazines with more fervour than ever. She read how one of the highest-paid New York models went to bed by eleven every night so that at her modelling appointments the next morning, she'd be fresh and energetic; not the kind of lifestyle you'd imagine a model leading at all. What about the parties, the invitations? Aileen wondered. She used her first pay cheque from Simpsons to purchase an elaborate supply of make-up from the store's Cosmetic Department and that night experimented with blue eyeshadow and went to bed early. Today she was wearing more make-up than usual but it had been applied carefully.

In Ralph's kitchen, Aileen drank a glass of water and checked her face in the mirror above the sink. He was edgy today; his wife was still in the hospital—the baby was almost due. He was in the living room telling her a joke. At first Aileen didn't get it. She had never heard the slang word "tool" before.

From the bedroom dresser drawer, he brought out three brassières and some of his wife's bikini pants.

"These'll do for the swimsuit shots," he said. "'bout your size?" He held them up, stretching the elastic waist of the pants.

Aileen let her breath out. She wanted to say no, or ask him if it was really necessary—" I'd rather not"—but something made her hesitate; in a way, she didn't want to say no. Although it frightened her, she rather liked the idea of adding to the repertoire of experience and wild, half-crazy, half-hazardous adventure she had begun. And it was difficult to know where to draw the line. She had no choice but to trust him; anyhow she was curious to see what she would look like in the camera's eye, wearing underwear. The idea of it titillated her. Someday she might be featured in the lingerie section of a catalogue.

On the bar stool, with Ralph standing across the room, his legs astride, one hand on his low-slung belt, waiting for her to go into a freeze, Aileen felt ridiculous for a moment. Nothing came to mind. Then, the pose she had assumed in her bedroom mirror at home came to mind and she flung her head back, letting her hair fall like soft, feathery ribbons against the small of her back, one toe off the stool's rung and pointed.

"Great!" Ralph said.

His wife was smaller. As Aileen arched her back, one breast slipped up and out of the cup. Her nipple caught on the edge of the brassiere and stayed there.

"Hold it," Ralph said, releasing the shutter.

He came up silently and lifted both of Aileen's breasts from the brassiere and let them sit on top of the cup. He ran his fingernail over each nipple till they were both hard and distended.

Aileen uttered a low throaty laugh which seemed caught somewhere; she had not moved when he instructed her not to. A good model follows instructions, she thought.

He went into the bedroom then and returned with a red silk brocade jacket and had her take the bra and panties off. She had never undressed in front of him before. She decided, without seeing the decision pass through her mind in the stages her decisions normally did, to undress with an air of ease, an air of efficiency.

"I don't want any crotch shots," she joked, unhooking the bra.

"No, no more of the breast either; nothing sexy about that."

He adjusted the spotlight and then the jacket, not saying a word but working with an air of professional nonchalance that Aileen felt grateful for; he lifted one breast inside the fold of the jacket so that it barely showed when she sat sideways. He draped her hair across her face and shoulder so that only the skin of her breast was visible. She felt better then. No one would know it was me, she told herself.

"How do you like these?" Aileen said, coming into her parents' living room with a selection of shots taken at the lake; she had chosen a few upper torso shots.

"They're not bad," Mr. Mason said, looking through them, passing a few across to his wife. He held one up to the lamp to see it better. "We're leaving this whole thing up to your own good judgement," he added turning to face Aileen. "I wouldn't expect you to look on it as a permanent job."

She nodded weakly, and felt herself running pale. She hadn't talked to her father lately; only about her mother's complaints, sometimes about things at his work, or her school. He was not one to complain but she knew he hated his job, the work he had been doing for twenty years now—lineman work. He wanted his children to pursue their education, to succeed where he had not. Aileen used to go buy him breakfast on Saturday and Sunday mornings, warbling in a loud, off-key voice: "I am a lineman for the county, and I drive the main road," just to make him laugh. And being able to suffer the work depended on that—his life at home. An uneasy force stirred in Aileen's body. The posing felt entirely comfortable in Ralph's presence, but now, as she vaguely considered the career she had embarked on, and her commitment to it, Aileen felt bewildered.

She didn't show the new set of pictures to anyone this time. They were ludicrous for the most part; she didn't feel herself to be alluring in them at all. She wondered if Mrs. Brown had delivered her baby yet and whether the woman would know that someone had been wearing her clothes. There was no way of guessing and either way, what did it matter if she did find out.

For a few weeks, Ralph did not call. Aileen wanted

to call him and yet faltered—she had never heard him be unwelcoming or abrupt, but something warned her that he had that capacity. It was just that she was looking particularly good these days; a professional artfulness had taken over her features which shocked her at times when she walked past a mirror or shiny glass window and saw the polished, poised and beautiful face that was hers. It irked her that Ralph was not capturing it, but she hesitated to be the one to call. She tried to figure out why he would put her off, be so thoughtless. She watched the paper's birth announcements and wondered about the Mid-Village Mall modelling assignment; it occurred to her that Ralph might have offered it to his other model. Meanwhile, another photographer had been looking her up. He had met her in Simpsons; said he had been struck by her face while he was riding the escalator to the second floor.

* * *

On Friday evening, in her bedroom after school, Aileen sat and looked through the window to her backyard; the mid-November ironwood and beech trees were almost skeletal. Their leaves, like so many yellow and orange Halloween candy wrappers, were raked into piles about the lawn. A few years ago I would have gone out and looked for leaves to preserve, the most perfect, the most haunting purple leaf I could find, Aileen thought. She was calculating the evening ahead, the weekend ahead, but the sudden memory of her girlhood taste for autumn pushed its way into the front of her mind, and then was gone.

Her parents' house was quiet with the kind of stillness that drove Aileen to distraction anymore, a heavy, smothering silence. It forced one to think, to grow depressed. Aileen left her room and walked down the hall to the living room where her mother was putting in time before starting the dinner; it was going to be late because Mr. Mason had been called out to an emergency. Somebody's power was dead.

"I'm going out—I'll have supper somewhere else," Aileen announced. Her mother turned away without protesting. She had virtually stopped speaking to Aileen altogether.

Downtown, the streets at six o'clock were still peaceful. The stores had barely closed for the evening but many of the front windows were still bright. Aileen walked slowly up the central street, stopping for long moments before each window. In Laura Secord's, a small white toy truck brimming with suckers and caramel candies, had a sign by it: "The Family that laughs together, stays together." Aileen smiled wryly. She rarely thought of her family now. Her mother had grown impossibly suspicious. It was difficult, as well, being the kind of salesgirl Simpsons wanted: an enterprising, award-winning company girl, a representative. For the most part, she isolated herself from the other salesgirls who were already banking on full-time, lengthy positions inside the store. Aileen felt above them, beyond them, even though there was nothing substantial to go on yet—not one of the modelling pictures, except the initial promotional one, had been displayed anywhere in town. She felt as if Ralph had let her down somehow and yet she was inextricably bound to him now.

A group of people, stragglers of the sort one saw early on an evening drifting about downtown, had assembled at the far end of the block. Aileen regarded them with little curiosity. She considered joining them briefly to see what spectacle they were being entertained by, but continued walking slowly, stopping once to check the amount of change her purse carried. At seven, she would phone a friend and meet her later for a movie. She was hungry; the Chinese restaurants smelled of plum sauce and french fries.

Once, she caught herself watching her own reflection as it approached her in a slanted store window. She slowed down and enjoyed the image. If only Ralph would chance by and see her looking this fine. I really should give him a call, Aileen thought. It was a waste to go unphotographed these days, just when she had finally pulled it all together, used the fashion magazines and make-up to such effectiveness. There wasn't a day passed that she didn't find herself in a pose—it could be in a chair, at her desk, walking across a lawn—and she knew, felt instinctively with her evolving set of appraising eyes, that she was exquisitely photogenic at that precise moment. She would definitely call him; he might have even attempted to contact her and been treated coolly by her parents. It was doubtful that he would be unreceptive. Perhaps her failure to call him had, in fact, suggested her disinterest. She could propose a meeting time, explain that she had been studying *Vogue* and *Glamour* for original new poses. Not a word about his silence for the past few weeks. She was angry but she could disguise that without completely giving in to him. Aileen quickened her pace, pleased by her plan.

She was at the end of the block, near the crowd, when something snapped at her attention; her heart began to beat erratically. Somehow, she knew, as she inched her way forward past the other spectators, what they were all watching; it simply came to her and a bulky, sinking weight of fear clutched her stomach. She stood behind a tall man, unnoticed amid the mostly hushed crowd, and along with the rest of them, watched her own father moving about the small area of the road that had been cleared of cars and people. It must have been the fallen wire, hissing now and moving like some venomous desert snake, that alerted her, that had warned her what the crowd, anxious and evil, had gathered to watch. She had heard the sound of the lines. She stared at her father for a minute, terrified that he might turn and spy

178

her—one of his tormenting audience—but he was occupied by his work. His head was bowed and he was working with tools, clumsily, because his hands were immersed in enormous, asbestos-stiff gloves. Aileen bowed her head, suddenly fearful that some stranger might recognize her. "Hey, isn't that the girl whose picture was..." Her father would notice, look up and see her and the situation would be worse because he would know that she hadn't spoken. He would know why. She filed out of the crowd, tripping over feet, and without turning back to see who was watching, retraced her steps. She had made up her mind. She had noticed a red telephone booth a few blocks on the other side of town. It was a chance worth taking.

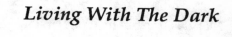

Living With The Dark

Meryl is lying beneath a Persian carpet. It is black under the carpet, but there are indeterminate murmurs and small clanging noises coming from the great expanse of the store, so the lights must still be on. They haven't locked up yet. The underside of the carpet smells old, dusty, rough. Meryl reaches up in the heavy, airless darkness and scratches her nose.

She has never broken a law before, other than minor ones—a speeding ticket here, a parking ticket there. Once, at university, she was caught shoplifting a steak and a bag of carrots from a grocery store but she cried and since stealing was not yet fashionable, the manager was sympathetic and let her go.

She wonders how the legal texts might phrase this particular crime. She has not broken and entered. Perhaps this is trespassing, perhaps not. She will get off on a technicality—as long as she is careful to conceal the bauble she will almost definitely be lifting before the night is over. A keepsake. She has dimly foreseen various results—a court room, a fine, a jail sentence, exposure, notoriety, her family's fury, her friends' initial bewilderment and eventual evaporation from her life. But she won't get caught. She has her plan and knows that the night will be an adventure that will fade in her mind like an overly brief summer holiday or an extraordinary dream.

She has pushed down the other thoughts—the courtroom, severe judge, severe jury thoughts. She has thought about other possibilities—getting frightened and wanting to leave, wanting to re-enter the world outside, the sidewalk world, the peopled, honking, fresh-air, real world beyond the revolving front door of the store. She might panic at some notion that insinuates itself like a snake into her mind and she might run past a supra-modern tractor beam alarm. There might even be a night security guard who will spy her shadow before she spies his, whispering triumphantly into his walkie-talkie, a direct line to the gloat of authorities, to sirens and flashing lights. The headlight of a car outside may pierce the glass of the revolving door and land on Meryl as she passes by, unwitting, dragging her feet on the fine old hardwood of the store's main floor, in a trance, sleepy for staying up all night long, mesmerized and drunk on the wafts of perfume and silk scarfs enveloping her.

She realizes that the murmurs have ceased; the clanking sounds of cash registers being emptied by slick, officious hands have stopped. Only one set of feet have tapped past the rug department in the last half hour— someone's final, unlooking check past the assortment of heaped and rolled-up rugs. Meryl sits up, sucking in her breath to summon the strength to lift the heavy Persian carpet lying across her chest and head. She disentangles her feet in the darkness—a semi-darkness, there are tiny night-lights glowing at the store's fire exits. She stands up, victorious, elated, shivering. She has a brief but profound wave of dizziness, such as she experiences frequently these days. It is from not sleeping, from drinking alone. It is PMS or anemia. It is from living beyond the pale.

She removes her shoes to walk down the frozen metal stairs—in case there is a security guard, or some advanced technological device that registers unusual sounds as part of its alarm system. How do old stores like this one with its back corridors and antechambers, its hardwood floors and dust, keep the place rid of mice? Of insects—moths that might ravage the expensive coats? She stops at each floor on her descent and listens. A sharp, frightening line of excitement runs up her spine and through her abdomen.

On the second floor, she walks through the pale half-light, reminiscent of scenes she has struggled to see on black-and-white tvs or of movies set at night where the murder and subsequent chase are frustratingly obscured by shadows. She fingers a camisole in the lingerie section. Intricately cut lace borders the satin cloth that gleams what must be ivory in the strange light. She hesitates and then takes off her sweater, then her bra, and slips the satin camisole over her head. Her toes curl into the thick pile rug beneath. She looks down at the camisole and wonders whether to wear it as she descends the marble staircase to the main floor. She waits for her first decision in this experiment to formulate itself.

She is certain that there is no guard in the store; she would sense him, hear him. He would walk boldly, make noise, whistle or hum—do any of the things that someone blithe and oblivious might do to put in time. Men whistle to put in time, or when they are frightened or bored. It is something Meryl has noted more than once. She is certain that the store does not employ a night security guard—but she has a sensation in her lower back, a pinging, electrical surge that is unpleasant, a warning. She has lost touch in the past few years with her instincts, her intuition—the forces that preserved her through childhood, through her teens, her twenties. She no longer knows which of her voices to listen to, cannot recall precisely what the core murmur sounds like, tastes like in her throat. She is not sure how the warning in her lower back translates into words.

She descends the marble staircase. She stops

abruptly and her fingers wrap around the banister. The store is lit by the outside world, by its streetlights and traffic. In planning, she visualized moving through near-darkness tonight. She looks down at the satin camisole, gleaming in the reflected light like a beacon. Something moves in the corner of her eye. Meryl suppresses a scream. She leans forward slightly and stares into the shadows and angles of the cosmetics section, then the accessories, then the men's wear department. Her eyes fall on a group of mannequins, immaculately perfect men with life-like postures and gestures, their features immobile and sleek, slick, imperturbable. One of them may have moved—the one dressed in sportswear, a light-coloured sweater draped across his shoulders, sleeves fastened around his neck and draping down his chest over a short-sleeved shirt. It is all too easy to invent a threat and terrify herself into submission, a change of heart, when nothing threatening exists—and she, who as a child happily imagined being locked in Tussaud's Chamber of Horrors for a night.

She goes to the perfume section first and looks for her favourite scents. The silvery half-light confounds her. She feels disappointed, thwarted by the reality of the situation. It will be difficult, she realizes, to play with the makeup and do herself over when the unnatural light of the city's street is leaching the colour from things, the very texture and weave of eye shadow and blush. Fortunately, she knows where on the counter to find Ysatis, Anais-Anais, and Diva. Her fingers would know their shapes in pitch dark. She often comes into the store to sample the perfumes on her way to the public school where she teaches her grade four class. The children are forthright and rude. They identify the perfumes aloud. It is part of her success at living that Meryl can now smile back agreeably and mask the roar of voices arguing inside her chest and throat.

She finds the Ysatis and sprays her left hand, then

185

liberally, her wrist and entire left arm. Finding the Diva, she does the same with her right side. The air becomes incensed around her. In the morning, the clerks meandering in from the early morning sunny street will stop in their tracks and wonder at the pervasive and lingering aroma. She finds the Anais-Anais and sprays her neck and exposed chest and wonders what she will eat for breakfast. She considers, playfully, the idea of remaining, of making a home here—a phantom of the Department store.

Her mirth disturbs the silence. But really—she could do this. How many days would pass until someone discovered she was a missing woman? She has experimented with forays into the wilderness before—two-day flights into snowy towns in the Laurentians to check into motels and look out the windows at the mountains, the brilliant sky that makes all life insignificant. To the Townships and down farmers' lanes to dead ends. Up the Richilieu River to gaze at century houses. And on her forays outside of the pale, she has searched through her car window into people's yards and verandas and the shapes of their homes trying to glean how they live; another way to live. In the middle of such nights, she casts a line for sleep and catches nothing but images of her life swirling, medieval existences, tortures in which she re-lives each nameless victim's agony, her own death, her own removal. She looks down the expanse of the nightened store and wonders about remaining forever.

By adjusting a mirror at the Lancome counter, Meryl can see her face quite clearly. She regards herself for a moment, wishing that her face would smile back. Her face is distorted, not its usual self. She has the unsettling, never-before-felt sensation of looking at someone outside of herself, a separate entity living in the mirror. She picks up a tiny brush and dabs it into a tray of sample blushes, eye shadows, lipsticks, mascaras. She is normally very pale. A touch of colour will make things look happier. She moves over to the Estee Lauder and at first carefully, then recklessly, applies eye shadow. She feels outraged by the lighting; she cannot tell colour. She realizes that she has always believed each colour felt different when it lay against her skin. She moves to the Shiseido and puts on lipstick which she is confident is bright red. She has been increasingly wary of painting herself up too garishly. But here, there is utter freedom. It is her own judgments she must hear out and contend with. She sprays her face and hair with Evian aerosol water and immediately feels better.

It is then that something near the back of the store moves. It might be the sound of a book being partly removed from one of the shelves in the book department that runs overhead along the right side of the store, or of a shoe tapping once and stopping, or of a purse relaxing, caving inwards infinitesimally as its leather creases and ages. Meryl walks over to the accessories department and ties a silk scarf around her neck. She puts on earrings, a bracelet and then an elaborate, darkly coloured, velvet bow in her hair. Slowly, silently, she pulls an umbrella from its floor-case, the one with the longest, brightest steel point.

It is not what she imagined, this evening spent locked inside the famous old department store, with all the time in the world to daub on exorbitantly expensive makeup and lotion, try on clothes—silks, cottons, designer rags, Italian shoes. Perhaps read one of the expensive coffee-table books in the book department overhead within the illumination cast from some richly scented candle. Open one of the boxes of Godiva chocolates and let the rich dark chocolate melt over her waxed and shining lips before slipping it into her mouth, explosions of elegant, out-of-reach flavour and touch.

It is not what she predicted; she is running out of things to do. She is tired. And something has moved at

187

the back of the store, something has shifted of its own volition. This is perhaps a regular event that people merely overlook, don't hear when it happens in real time, in day time, in the safety and deception of daylight. Or don't observe when things have been shut off, because they have followed suit and shut themselves off, shut themselves up and away, asleep, their alarms turned on, their escape from the world.

There is a rustling sensation along one of the store aisles. Past the makeup and the jewelry, past the borderline of the men's furnishings. Perhaps the store indeed has mice. Perhaps a breeze is blowing in from one of the vents and a piece of cloth is waving gently. A sheaf of paper has slipped off a sales desk and has floated down like a leaf to the floor. Meryl peers through the gloom of the store's interior. She glances down at her arm suddenly, startled at a tattoo that has appeared on her right forearm, an intricate mosaic, a wild rose, a storming sky, a shape sculpted by the forces of nature. She takes a step forward, still admiring her arm. The tattoo evaporates as the light falling in through the windows in the doors is left behind her. She steps backwards and the skin embroidery reappears. She looks up smiling and frowning. She considers getting a tattoo tomorrow, somewhere hidden. She gazes along the aisle, imagining a tattoo, and sees a dark figure move among the racks of men's housecoats and dinner jackets.

Her legs buckle and she finds herself squatting, trembling. She walks bent over to sidle in behind a counter of gloves. The smell of soft kid leather floats over her head. She has experienced this before—trying to listen intently into the black silence of a mid-night apartment, house, or hotel room, and hearing the quietness distort until it sounds as if an orchestra is playing, a riot is waging, an angry traffic jam is spilling over into violence. She presses herself from the inside out to extend her hearing as she has done in the past, bolting her doors and lying awake alongside her fear of who and what and when, a feeling she lives with always now, figures most women must, those who are alone.

He will have seen her, she realizes. She has been able to detect the slightest shuffle, his shadow moving obscurely in the depths of the store. Stupidly, she has sprayed perfume leaving the sound and the smell around her, she has walked down the stairs wearing the camisole like a country's arrogant flag. She has been talking to herself as well, no doubt.

She glances behind her through a partition in the counter to the revolving doors and the main street beyond. People are walking past the doors. She sees someone's head turn, glance into the dark nether regions of the store, and look ahead again. There are honks, a brief siren. She could run to the revolving door and leave the store. But it will be locked and she might have trouble finding the bolt in this darkness. And outside on the sidewalk—she may be seen leaving the store, by a citizen or by police. And she has no idea how peculiar her face looks. She is not ready for questions and tests, injections and specialists. She is not unable. She has merely stepped outside of things to take a breather and consider. I am innocent, she says.

To be ready for whatever is about to happen, she pulls her sweater back over her head and stuffs her bra into the back pocket of her jeans. The hard sales tag of the camisole presses into the space between her shoulder blades like incisors.

She fingers the steel point of the umbrella and looks several yards away to a glass show case containing paperweights. She has often stopped, after trying on perfume and sampling lotions, to peer through the glass at these precious objects, fantastic layers of glass and prism and the petals of vividly coloured orchids and butterflies. She considers going over to the counter now and removing one of those paperweights, using it to

189

throw with. She has never been very good at throwing things.

This time, his movement is far more audible. He isn't even trying now to disguise himself, his presence. It occurs to her that her adventure, her fading-into-ridiculous idea of many weeks, may have been shared by someone else. What if someone else has hidden in the store tonight? It may even be something that happens regularly, goes undetected, or unreported so that the temptation does not become epidemic. Meryl remembers freezing on the marble staircase and the tingling pain in her lower back, her eyes falling on the men's-wear mannequins. Perhaps one of them was real, an intruder like herself, doing something different, something special, searching for uniqueness, posturing on the dais of plastic models to look unreal as Meryl's own footsteps descended the stairs.

A thirst begins in her throat such as she has rarely experienced in the past, once hiking through the hot, airless dunes of Sand Banks Park with a man who refused to carry the overloaded bags she had brought for a picnic, another time after lying in a recovery room following an abortion. She has trouble swallowing and her eyes seem to be following suit, drying up. She licks her lips to remove some of the thick lipstick and swirl it in her mouth.

His footsteps tread softly along the main corridor of the store, between the gleaming mirrors and displays, the exquisite objets d'art, the rich tapestries and books. He, of course, is not frightened of her. He may even have entertained himself by imagining this very development in his adventure—a woman. Peering from beneath the counter, Meryl strains to listen, to see his feet. He is wearing running shoes, long pants. She can hear his breath ever so lightly, the moistening sound of his lips, his hand brushing past his clothing. She almost wishes that he would speak—utter at least one word so that the sensation of unreality coursing through her heart would end and she could run, be pursued, smash one of the revolving doors, scream for help.

He stops, listening likely, knowing too—and then continues. When he leans over at the revolving door to unlatch the bolt, Meryl lays her head sideways so that her cheek settles into the warp of the rug and she is able to see the dark shape that is him, his arm a light patch wrenching. The bolt snaps back with an iron crack. He stands again and there is a swish, a draught of cool air, the noise of the city and then relative silence once more.

Meryl sits up. She stands and, taking a kleenex from a box on the counter, wipes her mouth. A feeling that she has almost forgotten, a ripping and red wave through her body, crushes her as she looks back into the empty store. Someone else has been here. He has seen her, observed her ridiculous behaviour, her compulsive play at the makeup counter. Someone has chosen this night, of all nights, to secret himself away in the store. She has perhaps ruined his night, prevented him from living out some greater plan, a major heist. Or perhaps he is routinely a fixture of the store and this is indeed where he makes his home, hangs his hat.

Meryl takes a long shawl from a rack and wraps it around her shoulders. She stands by the revolving door only long enough to watch the street and ensure that a cruiser is not at that moment pulling up at the intersection. She pushes through the door and lets it fall behind her unlocked and then she sees him—a dark shadow three blocks to the west by now, heading for somewhere. Uncertain, she takes a few steps after him, and then begins to lightly run.

191

Printed in Canada